Anastasia,
Absolutely

D0204046

OTHER YEARLING BOOKS BY LOIS LOWRY YOU WILL ENJOY:

NUMBER THE STARS
ANASTASIA KRUPNIK
ANASTASIA AGAIN!
ANASTASIA AT YOUR SERVICE
ANASTASIA, ASK YOUR ANALYST
ANASTASIA ON HER OWN
ANASTASIA HAS THE ANSWERS
ANASTASIA'S CHOSEN CAREER
ANASTASIA AT THIS ADDRESS
ALL ABOUT SAM
ATTABOY, SAM!
AUTUMN STREET
TAKING CARE OF TERRIFIC
YOUR MOVE, J.P.!
RABBLE STARKEY

YEARLING BOOKS are designed especially to entertain and enlighten young people. Patricia Reilly Giff, consultant to this series, received her bachelor's degree from Marymount College and a master's degree in history from St. John's University. She holds a Professional Diploma in Reading and a Doctorate of Humane Letters from Hofstra University. She was a teacher and reading consultant for many years, and is the author of numerous books for young readers.

For a complete listing of all Yearling titles, write to
Dell Readers Service,
P.O. Box 1045
South Holland, IL 60473

Anastasia,
Absolutely

Lois Lowry

A Yearling Book

Published by
Bantam Doubleday Dell Books for Young Readers
a division of
Bantam Doubleday Dell Publishing Group, Inc.
1540 Broadway
New York, New York 10036

If you purchased this book without a cover you should be aware that this book is stolen property. It was reported as "unsold and destroyed" to the publisher and neither the author nor the publisher has received any payment for this "stripped book."

Copyright © 1995 by Lois Lowry

All rights reserved. No part of this book may be reproduced or transmitted in any form or by any means, electronic or mechanical, including photocopying, recording, or by any information storage and retrieval system, without the written permission of the Publisher, except where permitted by law. For information write to Permissions, Houghton Mifflin Company, 215 Park Avenue South, New York, New York 10003.

The trademarks Yearling® and Dell® are registered in the U.S. Patent and Trademark Office and in other countries.

ISBN: 0-440-41222-6

Reprinted by arrangement with Houghton Mifflin Company

Printed in the United States of America

April 1997

10   9   8   7   6   5   4   3   2

CWO

Anastasia,
Absolutely

1

"Anastasia!"

"Hunh?" Anastasia opened her eyes groggily. Her bedroom was dark and she couldn't remember at first what day it was. But she recognized the voice. It was her mother's voice, and it was angry.

There was another sound, too — a kind of crying, as if someone had left a baby on the doorstep. *Great*, Anastasia thought, as she sat up in bed; *that's all we need: a baby on our doorstep, with a pathetic little note pinned to its undershirt.*

"*Anastasia!*" Her mother was at the foot of the stairs that led to Anastasia's third-floor bedroom. "Wake up!"

"I'm awake," Anastasia called. "What's going on? What's that crying?" She went to the top of the stairs, looked down through the dim light, and saw her mother standing there in the over-sized Harvard sweatshirt she usually wore instead of a nightgown.

"That crying is your *dog*, remember?" her mother asked loudly. "Your dog that you are going to take care of, that you are going to get up with every morning, remember?

1

You promised, Anastasia. You promised at least forty times before we agreed to take on this dog, and last night after dinner you promised once again!"

"Yeah." *Dog. Yes. Dog.* Now she remembered.

"Today," Mrs. Krupnik called, as the whining and crying became louder, "is the first day of the rest of your life."

"I know! I'm coming!" Quickly Anastasia reached for her glasses and a pair of sweatpants that were draped on a chair. She pulled them on over her pajamas, found some dirty socks on the floor, and pulled those on as well.

"Here I am!" She dashed down the stairs from her third-floor room. "I'm sorry. I didn't hear him at first. Actually, I heard him, but I thought somebody had left a baby on our doorstep."

"A what?"

"A baby, with a note saying 'Please take care of me.' "

Her mother stared at her for a moment, and then shook her head. "I am going back to bed," she announced wearily, and headed back toward the bedroom where Anastasia's father was still asleep. Anastasia could see him there, a big mound under the blankets.

"What's that scary noise?" Sam's voice came from his bedroom. Anastasia poked her head through his half-opened door and said soothingly, "Shhh. Go back to sleep. It's just the dog."

Sam, who was sitting up in bed, lay back down, rolled over, and closed his eyes. Mrs. Krupnik had gone back into the master bedroom and closed the door. The mound that was Anastasia's father hadn't moved. Myron Krupnik slept through everything. He complained that he missed a lot of

2

interesting stuff because of it. Just last month their neighbor, Mr. Fosburgh, who couldn't seem to quit smoking even though he had tried about four hundred times, had set fire to his living room curtains and three fire engines had come with their sirens full blast. It was the most exciting event in their neighborhood in years, and Myron Krupnik had slept through the entire thing.

It was truly amazing, though, Anastasia thought, that Dad was sleeping through this. The dog was howling now, and he was scratching loudly at the door to the room where he was confined, the little unused room at the end of the second floor hall.

When the Krupniks had moved to this house the year before, they had argued about that room.

"It's a sewing room," Anastasia's father had said.

"Excuse me?" his wife replied. "A sewing room? Did you intend that I be enclosed up there, maybe stitching fine linen shirts by hand for my master, or darning his socks and underwear? Am I hearing you correctly?"

Myron Krupnik had backed off quickly. "No," he said. "I lost my head. It is definitely not a sewing room."

"Maybe it could be a workroom for Dad," Anastasia suggested. "For his hobbies."

Her parents had looked at her quizzically. Her father was an English professor. On the first floor of the house was a large bookcase-lined study, where her father sat often in the evenings, reading, correcting papers, listening to music.

"What hobbies?" her father had asked, with a very curious look.

3

"Ah, woodworking?" Anastasia suggested tentatively.

"*Woodworking?*" Mr. Krupnik didn't sound irritated, just puzzled.

"Making birdhouses and stuff?"

"*Birdhouses?*"

"No, I guess not," Anastasia admitted. He was right. Her dad was not a hobbies kind of guy.

"Maybe it could be a hideout room," Sam had suggested.

They had all looked at him. "For if bad guys come," Sam explained, "and need a hideout? We could put them in there, and they could shoot their guns out the window." He aimed one of his fingers and made a few *pft-pft* shooting sounds.

No matter how often the entire family tried to deflect Sam's interest in guns, tried to direct him to peaceful ways of resolving conflict, he always found a way back to Uzis and bazookas. "No hideout, Sam," Mrs. Krupnik said firmly. "No bad guys. No guns."

"Well," Anastasia had proposed finally, "it would make a good room for a dog to sle — "

"No," her mother had said.

"No," her father had said.

"Rats," Anastasia had said.

But that had been a year ago. And now they had a dog, and now the little room had become The Dog's Room — because the dog didn't even have a name yet — and Anastasia had promised faithfully that she would feed the dog, train the dog, clean up after the dog, and walk the dog regularly, even early in the morning, though she had not realized until this minute that "early in the morning" might mean *dawn*, for pete's sake.

She opened the door to The Dog's Room. He leaped at her and licked her face.

"Hi," Anastasia said, and scratched him behind the ear. She yawned, the dog yawned, which made her yawn again, and then he scampered ahead of her, down the stairs, and stood waiting by the front door.

Funny, she thought, how this dog had never been in this house in his life until yesterday, but already he knew the layout. All by smell, too. He had so much shaggy hair in his eyes that Anastasia was quite certain he couldn't see anything. But he sniffed incessantly, leaning his head down and making his way around by following his nose. During his first hour in the Krupniks' house, he had discovered some stale cheese crackers on Anastasia's desk and a moldy half of a tuna fish sandwich that Sam had wedged behind a radiator.

"Not me," Sam had said, when they showed him. "Bad guys did it."

Now the unnamed dog stood impatiently by the front door as if he had lived in the house all his life and knew exactly which way was marked EXIT. When he heard Anastasia jiggling his leash in her hand, he quivered with anticipation and made an excited whimpering noise.

Hurry up, hurry up, he was saying. *My goodness,* Anastasia thought in surprise. *I can understand dog language.*

"In a minute," she told him. "Let me put my jacket on."

He wiggled, and said again, *Hurry up.*

5

Anastasia zipped her jacket, attached the leash to his collar, and unlocked the front door.

"Ooops," she said. "Forgot something. Just a minute." She reached over and picked up the thick padded envelope on the hall table. "I promised Mom I'd mail this. It's her sketches for a new book. Boy, she'd kill me if I forgot. They're already late and the publisher's been bugging her about it. And guess what — the book's about a dog."

Pleeeeeze hurry, the dog said, nudging the door with his nose. He didn't seem to be interested in hearing about Mrs. Krupnik's illustrations.

"One more thing. Plastic bag for you know what." It was the gross part, but Anastasia had promised her parents that she would clean up after the dog. She opened the front door, picked up her father's *New York Times* from the front steps, and removed it from its blue plastic bag. She tossed the paper onto the hall table and put the crumpled bag into her pocket. She just hoped that no one would see her, especially not Steve Harvey, who was in her class at school and also lived down the street, as she packaged dog poop in a plastic bag. Talk about embarrassing.

Finally she was ready. With her mother's mail in one hand, the plastic bag in a pocket, and holding the leash firmly to restrain the dog, who was tugging hard, Anastasia started out on the first morning of the rest of her life. *My Life with a Dog,* she thought, and liked the sound of it.

She glanced back at the hall clock before she closed the front door.

Good grief. It was still just 6:08. Anastasia yawned again and headed down the front steps into the dawn.

6

"My goodness, isn't he cute? What kind of dog *is* he?"

Anastasia smiled politely at the woman. It was amazing how many people were actually out here at sunrise: some of them walking their dogs, others jogging. This woman was wearing a jogging suit and was carrying weights in her hands and walking very fast, though she had stopped now to admire Anastasia's dog.

"Well, he's really a mutt," Anastasia explained. "Mixed breed, the vet calls it. He's part poodle and part Tibetan, and part Wheaten, and . . . I forget what else. But all the different *parts* are nonallergenic. My dad's allergic to dogs — and to cats, too — so we could never have a pet. My brother got a kitten and my dad promised to try not to sneeze, but he sneezed for five days straight, and now Sam's kitten has to live in the garage."

Suddenly Anastasia thought, *I'm talking too much, as usual. Why don't I ever know when to shut up? I am going to concentrate on that part of my personality: learning when to keep my mouth shut.*

But the woman did seem interested, so Anastasia went on.

"Then the vet called us — he's a friend of my dad's because they went to college together a million years ago — and said he had to find a home for this dog, and it was nonallergenic because it was a mix of lots of kinds of nonallergenic dogs."

The woman leaned over, shifted one of her weights to the other hand, and scratched the dog in the shaggy hair behind his ears. "What's his name?" she asked.

"He doesn't have one yet. We just got him. Actually, of course he *had* a name, but we're going to give him a new one. Only I have to think of just the right one."

" 'Shaggy,' " the woman suggested.

Anastasia made a face. "Thanks. But I don't think so. It's a little too obvious."

" 'Fuzzy' ?"

Great. The woman was going to stay there all morning, entering a dog-naming contest.

"Well, I'll give that some thought," Anastasia said politely. "But we're trying to think of a name that would sort of *sound* like his old name, so that it will seem a little familiar to him." She tugged on the leash and pulled the dog away. He sniffed at a hedge, raised his leg tentatively, thought better of it, and trotted forward along the side-walk.

The woman followed. "What's his old name?" she asked.

Anastasia sighed. She had been trying hard not to *say* the dog's previous name, because it was a stupid name and she wanted him to forget about it. But she didn't want to be rude. Finally, reluctantly, she whispered it to the woman. "Louie," she said, under her breath.

"Oh! So you need something with an *oooo* sound! How about 'Pookie'?"

"Thanks. That's really cute. I have to go now." Anastasia hurried along behind the dog, who was not under any circumstances in the entire world going to be named Pookie, and at last the woman waved and went away.

The sun was beginning to come up. Anastasia, approaching a corner where a brick building housed an insurance agency, exchanged smiles with a newspaper delivery person, two more joggers, and a man with two golden retrievers at his side. A woman with a tall thin dog on a red leash seemed very friendly. All of the people she passed did. They said things like "Good morning" or "Hi there" or "Nice day" or "Nice dog."

Actually, it was kind of fun becoming a morning person, Anastasia decided. And also, it gave you time to think. In real life, in the regular daytime hours, you never had time to think because you were so busy doing stuff.

And Anastasia needed to think. Back home, back on the desk in her bedroom, she had a school paper to write.

Many of the free periods that had been study halls or library time were now going to be devoted to Values, until Christmas. After Christmas Anastasia could go back to studying and reading and daydreaming and doodling again; but for now, from Monday to Friday each week, every single day, she would have to think about Values. She had groaned about it to her parents, but they hadn't been very sympathetic; they had pointed out that all human beings should be thinking about Values every single day of their life anyway.

The course had just begun, and the teacher, Mr. Francisco, had given them each a set of questions. Well, they weren't actually *questions;* they were sort of *situations.* Each of the students was supposed to write about how he or she would react in each situation.

Anastasia had thought it would be kind of boring and that she wouldn't have any problem with Values. After all,

9

she thought, she'd been brought up in a family with very good values. She had been quite certain that she knew exactly how she felt in any given situation and what the right response was.

But some of Mr. Francisco's hypothetical situations were a little complicated. They made her confused. That was why she needed time to think.

She'd already completed her answer to the first question — about whether she would be willing to smash a small groundhog over the head with a rock if it meant that by doing so she would save a vegetable garden that would feed a poor family for an entire summer. But it hadn't been easy, and even now she wasn't sure that she'd made the right choice. She thought she'd have to rewrite her answer.

For the first time in her life, Anastasia realized that she had trouble making important decisions.

I am an indecisive person, she thought. *Not only do I talk too much, but I am* wishy-washy. It was depressing, having so many serious flaws.

While Anastasia mused about groundhogs, values, and character deficiencies, she also thought about a name for the dog. Clearly he couldn't go on very long without a name; it wouldn't be fair. Anastasia remembered when her brother had been born, three years before, and they chose his name the very first day, when he was just about four hours old. Of course they had had about six months to think about it.

But the dog had been a sort of surprise. The vet called about him; they went to see him; Myron Krupnik didn't sneeze or itch; and so they had taken the homeless dog home, stopping en route at the store to buy some food and a dish. It had been quite sudden, with no time to come up with a name.

The dog continued to trot, stopping here and there to sniff. It was astonishing how curious a dog he was, Anastasia thought. Maybe his name should be Sniffer.

No. Sniffer wasn't it; it didn't have the *oooo* sound that they needed.

Anastasia knew that when she hit on the right name, it would be clear to her at once, like a light bulb appearing over someone's head in a comic book.

The dog stopped again, at the corner, and examined a grassy square around a lamppost carefully.

Snoopy?

No. That name was, well, *used*.

Finally the moment came, the moment Anastasia had dreaded, the moment when she had to scoop. She glanced quickly around; the woman with the red-leashed dog was still nearby but looking in another direction. Luckily there were few people around. The main observer was the dog, who seemed very interested in the blue newspaper bag, as if he were thinking, *Why on earth would you do that?*

Anastasia was wondering the same thing. But dutifully, because she had promised her parents she would, she scooped the unattractively large and surprisingly steamy mound into the plastic bag that only thirty minutes before had held her father's *New York Times*.

Scooper? That was a name with an *oooo* sound.

No. No light bulb appeared.

Pooper?

No way.

Anastasia sighed. *I'm so wishy-washy*, she thought, *that I can't even name a dog*.

Fortunately no one was really watching while she scooped. She had dreaded scooping in front of onlookers. But there was one exception — a man who scowled at her. *If he's that grouchy seeing me scoop it up*, Anastasia thought, *I wonder how he would have looked if I* hadn't.

Flustered because the man was still looking — and because the dog had growled slightly at him, the only time she had ever heard a growl issue from the dog's mouth, but she didn't really blame him because he really deserved privacy in such circumstances, and it wasn't fair of the guy to look — Anastasia hastily mailed her mother's packet of sketches in the corner mailbox. Then she glanced at her watch, which said 6:32. *Darn it*. She decided reluctantly that she would not, after all, be able to go back to bed.

Walking home, the dog continued to stop and sniff and examine. Everything seemed to be of intense interest. He analyzed the shape of a rock in the gutter. Then he pawed at a crumpled paper, studied it closely for a moment, and tasted it meticulously. He inspected a dead leaf with care. He nudged a twig and turned it over with an investigatory paw. It was almost as if he were a detective, looking for clues of some sort. As if he were a —

SLEUTH.

The light bulb appeared! It had the *oooo* sound she needed. Anastasia grinned and tried it out on the dog.

"Come, Sleuth," she said. He looked up, cocked his head, and sauntered cheerfully over to where she stood.

"Onward, Sleuth," she commanded, and they continued along.

Now and then the shaggy dog stopped to raise his leg. He marked his places along the way, as if, newly named, he needed to reidentify his turf. *This is my neighborhood,* he was saying. *Watch out, world.* Sleuth *lives here.*

VALUES

1. *Suppose that in order to protect and save a small vegetable garden that would feed a hungry family for an entire summer, you were required to hit a groundhog over the head with a rock and kill it. Would you do so?*

Although I like animals a lot (I have a dog, myself) I think human beings are more important, in the great scheme of things. And even though I basically don't believe in harming living creatures, if I absolutely had to, I guess I would kill a groundhog.

But first I would have to be absolutely positive that it was the groundhog that was eating the vegetables. I mean, what if maybe it was actually something else, maybe a person or something, maybe even a *starving* person who was sneaking in at night and stealing vegetables, and making it look as if a groundhog was doing it?

And even if it *was* definitely a groundhog, why would I have to kill it with a rock? I mean, couldn't you give it a painless shot or something?

I guess I don't think it would exactly be *right* to

kill it, even with a painless shot, but it would be *righter* than letting a whole family starve to death.

Even though I don't believe they actually would. They could get food from dumpsters behind the supermarket, if they had to. Or the Salvation Army would help.

2

"I named him!" Anastasia announced, dashing into the kitchen after she had unhooked the dog's leash and hung it with her jacket in the hall closet. "His name is Sleuth! It's because he sniffs at everything, like a detective. Like Colombo! And it has the *oooo* sound!"

"I like it," Mrs. Krupnik said. "*Sleuth*. Yes. It's good. But I hope tomorrow morning you'll hear him a little sooner, Anastasia. I don't want to have to get up and call you every morning."

"I'll try," Anastasia promised. She poured dry dog food into the dog's dish on the kitchen floor, beside the door to the pantry, and watched him gobble enthusiastically.

Then she sliced a banana into the bowl of raisin bran that her mother had set in her place at the breakfast table. In the corner of the kitchen, the dog curled up after eating his own breakfast and immediately fell asleep beside his bowl. It didn't seem quite fair that, after an early morning walk, and after a big bowl of dog food, now he got to go back to sleep while *she* had to go to school.

"Did you clean up after him?" her father asked, looking up from his *New York Times*.

Anastasia nodded. She gave her father a particular look, which meant to convey the message: *This is not a topic I care to discuss at breakfast.*

"What did you do with it?" Mrs. Krupnik asked.

Anastasia sighed and put down her spoon. "I put it in a plastic bag," she said patiently. "Actually, I used the plastic bag that your newspaper came in, Dad."

Myron Krupnik looked down at his newspaper. "Oh. I wondered why it was naked this morning," he said. "Well, fine. That's recycling, I guess."

Sam was stirring his oatmeal thoughtfully. He always played games with his oatmeal. "What did you put in the plastic bag?" he asked.

"Never mind," Anastasia told him.

"Then where did you put the plastic bag, Anastasia?" Her mother had gone to the counter to pour another cup of coffee.

The raisin bran had become less and less appealing now that her entire family seemed to be obsessed by the need to know more about the disposal of dog excrement than she had any interest in telling them. Anastasia put her spoon down and wiped her mouth on a paper napkin. She sighed. "I dropped it in the trash can in our garage," she said.

"*What* did you drop in the trash can?" Sam asked loudly.

"Never mind, Sam," said his mother. She sat back down with her second cup of coffee.

In the corner, Sleuth stirred. He raised his head, sniffed, stood up, sneezed, turned around in a circle, lay back down, and fell asleep again. Mrs. Krupnik looked over at him.

"I don't know," she said, a little uneasily. "It bothers me that he looks like a mop. If he had a handle sticking out of his back, you wouldn't be able to tell him from a dust mop. And I am not someone who enjoys having a mop in the corner of the kitchen. It makes me feel guilty for being a lousy housekeeper."

The dog yawned.

"Mops don't yawn," Anastasia reassured her mother.

"I don't think I've sneezed once in the twenty-four hours we've had him," Myron Krupnik announced. "I think it's going to work. And I like his name, Anastasia. Good choice. There was once a terrific play named *Sleuth*, incidentally. It had Laurence Olivier in it. And they made it into a great movie. I'll rent it for us sometime."

"Is it about a dog?"

"Nope," her father said. "It's about a sleuth."

"The dog sneezed, though," Sam pointed out. "He sneezed last night and he just sneezed again. Maybe he's allergic to us!"

"Dogs always sneeze," Anastasia said. "They sneeze when they're happy. My dog book explained that."

Sam stirred the last of his oatmeal and took a final bite. With his mouth full, he said, "But then how come there's a Sneezy and a Happy in the Seven Dwarfs? Because if you sneeze when you're happy, then Sneezy and Happy would be the same one, and — "

18

Anastasia interrupted him. "It's only that way with dogs, not dwarfs, Sam.

"By the way," she said, turning to her parents, "would you guys kill a groundhog if it were eating a garden that belonged to poor, hungry people?"

"I'd call the Humane Society," her mother said.

"I'd go to the hardware store and get a Havahart trap," her father said. "Then I'd trap it and let it loose someplace, maybe in New Hampshire or Vermont or something. Of course they wouldn't love that in New Hampshire or Vermont. Maybe I'd try to sell it to a pet store."

"*I'd* kill it," Sam said happily. "I'd shoot it with a shotgun. I'd blast its head right off." He aimed his toast at Anastasia and made a shooting sound. She noticed that he had bitten his toast carefully into the shape of a handgun.

"Maybe it could be a cute little pet, Sam," Anastasia suggested, hoping to enhance her brother's values. "You wouldn't shoot a pet, would you?"

Sam frowned. "No," he said. "I guess not." He ate the handgrip of his toast gun.

"But actually," Mrs. Krupnik said, stirring her coffee thoughtfully, "if a whole family was depending on that garden, maybe — "

Myron Krupnik looked up from his paper. "Killing wildlife for food isn't morally unsound," he commented. "Primitive societies do it all the time."

"But what if — " his wife began.

"*See?*" Anastasia wailed. "We're all of us indecisive! We ought to be named the wishy-washy family!"

Her mother's eyes lit up the way they sometimes did

when she was working on a particularly creative illustration. "What a great title for a children's book! *The Wishy-Washy Family*! No, wait. How about just: *The Wishy-Washies*? I might suggest that to a publisher. Wouldn't it — "

Anastasia groaned. "I have to feed Frank Goldfish and get dressed for school," she said. She took her bowl to the sink and started toward the stairs.

Instantly the dog, who had been snoring, was awake, alert, on his feet, and at her side.

"Okay, Sleuthie, come on," Anastasia said, laughing, and headed to her room.

Anastasia sat at her desk in Mr. Francisco's class and glanced surreptitiously at her watch. She didn't want to hurt the teacher's feelings, but Values was actually a pretty boring class. They had been discussing groundhogs for thirty-two minutes — no, thirty-*three* minutes actually, she thought, watching the hand on her watch face jump ahead. That was about thirty-one minutes more than she had ever thought in her entire life about groundhogs, up to now.

It was amazing how everybody in the eighth grade seemed to have had a groundhog experience at some time — and even more amazing how they seemed to want to describe it.

It reminded Anastasia of a day in second grade, six years ago, when she was only seven. A lady who wrote children's books had come to visit the classroom. She had brought with her a picture book that she had written about a zoo. And she had done the pictures (which she explained were called illustrations) in the book, too. She showed the original paintings of various animals and she showed the pages on which she had written the story, with all the crossed-out words, and she explained how she had rewritten it again and again. She told about how she chose the title: *Zoo Who*. Then she described how the book was published.

Finally, she asked if there were any questions. Every second grader in the room, including Anastasia, raised a hand.

The lady looked very pleased. She smiled. "Yes?" she said, and pointed to Jenny MacCauley.

"I went to the zoo," Jenny said, "and we saw a whole lot of monkeys, and they smelled really bad, and my mom said she didn't want to have lunch because the smell made her stomach feel sick."

"That's very interesting," the lady said. "I enjoyed doing the illustration of monkeys because they're so lively. Does someone have a question about writing books, or about my book? Yes? You over there, in the blue shirt." She pointed to Daniel Cirelli.

"I went to the zoo with my cousins," Daniel said. "And my cousin Joey? He kept punching me in the car, and his mom said if he didn't stop we wouldn't even be allowed to go to the zoo, and we'd go back home instead, so Joey — "

"Isn't it fun," the book-writing lady said, "to visit the zoo? I spent a lot of time at the zoo when I was doing the research for my book, *Zoo Who*." She held it up. "Who can guess how much research I needed to learn about all the

21

animals? Would you guess one day, or one week, or one month? You there with your hand up, in the yellow sweater." She pointed to Lindsay Cavanaugh.

"I went to the Franklin Park Zoo," Lindsay said, "and the elephant had a big scab on its leg."

Remembering the second-grade afternoon, Anastasia smiled. The lady hadn't called on her, even though she had her hand up, but she had wanted very much, she recalled, to tell about the time *she* had gone to the zoo.

And now the same thing was happening. Every student in Mr. Francisco's class wanted to tell about the time their uncle shot a groundhog, or their cousin poisoned a groundhog, or their next door neighbor whacked a groundhog over the head with a croquet mallet.

Anastasia had no interest in groundhogs, or any groundhogs tales to tell, and she thought the class was quite boring; but she did enjoy watching Mr. Francisco, who was extremely handsome.

He was new to the school. He was more patient than the other teachers. He was younger. He joked a lot, and knew the names of rock groups, and he'd seen movies like *Wayne's World,* which Anastasia assumed no adult had ever seen.

He was the kind of teacher a kid could be *friends* with. In fact, very recently Anastasia's friend Daphne Bellingham had gone to see Mr. Francisco in his office, after school, to explain that she hadn't done the assigned reading because she'd been visiting her father over the weekend and had forgotten to take the book with her. Daphne said that they'd sat there in his office talking like a couple

22

of equals, instead of the usual Powerful Teacher/Humble Student conversation that kids were accustomed to. In fact, Daphne confided, Mr. Francisco had said that while they were in his office — though never in class — Daphne could feel free to call him Barry.

Barry. Anastasia thought about the name, saying it to herself under her breath in class. It was an okay name, she guessed. Not great, but okay.

She wondered if he would say the same thing to her if she ever went to his office. "Call me *Barry*."

She couldn't respond "Call me Anastasia," because of course he already did call her Anastasia. So what would she say?

Just: "All right, Barry."

It felt a little weird. Even thinking about it felt a little weird. She decided that she wouldn't go to his office.

"Time's about up, guys," Mr. Francisco was saying. "Work on the second and third questions tonight. All those of you who think it's no big deal to murder a groundhog? You might find tonight's questions a little tougher."

The bell rang and the students picked up their books. Anastasia closed her notebook and headed toward the door to meet Daphne and Meredith. They had gym together the next period.

"Forget the stupid vegetable garden," she overheard Ben Barstow say to a group of his pals. "They oughta just eat the groundhog!"

"Protein! *Right! Yeah!*" the other boys responded enthusiastically. One of them began making loud chewing and slurping sounds.

23

Anastasia rolled her eyes in disgust, caught up with her waiting friends, and headed down the corridor.

"Cool name," Meredith said. "Sleuth. You're really lucky, Anastasia." They were in the cafeteria eating lunch after gym class. "I wish I could have a dog, but my mom hates them."

"My mother loves dogs," Daphne said, nibbling the cheese from the edge of a pizza slice, "but our dumb apartment building doesn't allow them. Remember my dog? Barkley? I only get to see him when I visit my father on weekends. He barely remembers me. Barkley, I mean, not my father. Boy, they talk about divorce hurting *kids*. How about *dogs*? Didn't anybody ever think about dogs?"

Sonja Isaacson, sitting next to Anastasia, poked her finger into the side of a Twinkie, squeezed slightly, and watched the cream filling ooze from the hole. She made a face and put the Twinkie down on her tray. "We have dogs," she reminded her friends, "but they really belong to my brothers. My brothers have to feed them and everything. My dad's always yelling at them because they forget."

"Dogs are a lot of work," Anastasia pointed out. "I had to promise to feed mine twice a day, and walk him twice a day. And he wakes up really early. This morning I was out on Chestnut Street with Sleuth and it was barely light. The sun was just coming up.

"Anybody want my chips?" she asked, looking at her tray and deciding that she'd eaten enough.

"Me. Thanks." Sonja leaned over and scooped up the

24

handful of potato chips. "If you were on Chestnut Street, did you see the police?"

"Yeah, *I* did," Meredith said, even though the question hadn't been meant for her. "I saw them on my way to school. There were millions of them. I bet anything somebody got murdered." She wadded up her paper napkin, aimed at the trash can, and tossed the napkin in. "Two points! Yay me," she said.

"There weren't millions, Mer," Daphne corrected. "You always exaggerate. There were two cruisers and four policemen out on the sidewalk. I saw them, too. I would have stopped to watch but I was already late for school."

Anastasia picked up her tray to take it to the window where empty trays and used utensils were returned. "What are you guys talking about?" she asked. "What police? I didn't see any police."

"On Chestnut Street, at the corner where that insurance agency is," Sonja described. "By the brick building with the parking lot? It was crawling with police at a quarter of eight this morning."

"No kidding." Anastasia balanced her tray in one hand and picked up her schoolbooks with the other. "Darn it. I was there about six-thirty. There's a mailbox on that corner. I mailed some stuff there, for my mom. But when I left for school later, I went the other way. I always miss everything interesting."

Sonja shrugged. "It wasn't all that interesting, actually. There wasn't a body or anything. The police were just standing around talking to each other."

"There weren't even any of those yellow ribbons tying off the crime scene," Meredith added.

"Nobody was handcuffed," Daphne said. "I looked at everybody's wrists when I went by."

"Well," Anastasia said, reassured that she hadn't missed a major event, "Sam would have loved it. All those policemen with guns."

"Hi, Sam. Whatcha doing?" Anastasia asked from the back steps. She had just arrived home from school, and her brother was coming through the kitchen door with something in his hand. "What do you have?"

Sam opened his fist and showed her the brown fish-shaped morsels. "Cat treats," he said. "I'm going to the garage to visit my kitten."

"I don't like looking at those, Sam," Anastasia said. "They make me think of Frank Goldfish."

Understandingly, Sam closed his hand so that she wouldn't have to view the cat treats.

Poor Sam. Anastasia felt sorry for him that his kitten now had to live in the garage, even though the kitten itself didn't seem to mind at all. Anastasia suspected there might be mice in the garage. The half-grown kitten was getting a little pudgy. "Uh-oh," Mrs. Krupnik had said, and asked the vet to check. But no, the kitten wasn't pregnant. It was a male kitten, and simply overeating. Probably it shouldn't even have the nasty-smelling little fish-flavored treats, Anastasia thought, but she didn't tell Sam that. He looked so cheerful, going for a visit to his pet.

"I'll come with you, okay?" She put her schoolbooks down on the porch steps.

"Okay," said Sam, and took Anastasia's hand in his own.

The gray kitten scampered out from behind some garden tools when they entered the garage, which was messy and dimly lit by the daylight filtered through cobwebbed windows. The Krupnik car now lived in the driveway so that the kitten could have a safe home; Anastasia's father said that it was the least he could do, to sacrifice his car's place, since it was he who was allergic to the kitten.

Sam squatted down and fed the treats to the kitten. Then he pulled a piece of string across the floor so that the kitten could chase it.

"What do you like best, cats or dogs?" Sam asked his sister.

"Both the same," Anastasia lied.

"Me too," Sam said cheerfully. "Both the same."

"I'm going to do a good deed for you, Sam. I'm going to empty the litter box," Anastasia said. She emptied the contents of the box into a plastic trash bag, twisted the top closed, and deposited it in the big trash can that stood by the garage door. She refilled the litter box from the bag of cat litter on a shelf.

Something created an odd little nudge of awareness in her mind. Something about the trash can.

"Here you are," she said to the kitten, putting the litter box back in its place on the ground near the plaid pillow that the cat used as a bed. "All set for another few days.

"Take it easy on the mice-munching, okay?" The kitten

cocked its head, twitched its ears, and looked at her alertly. Sam giggled.

There was *something* about the trash can. It was one of those feelings that you get. Something wasn't exactly right.

Anastasia tried to think about what she had put into the trash can recently. Oh. Of course. Her father's *New York Times* blue plastic bag, functioning as a pooper-scooper that very morning. She laughed a little to herself and wrinkled her nose.

But why did she feel something was *wrong?*

Anastasia went back to the trash can, lifted the lid, saw the bag of cat litter that she had just placed inside, thought briefly to herself that the poor trash can was turning into an outhouse, and made herself lift up the bag of used litter in order to assess what was underneath.

What was underneath was a mailing envelope addressed to a New York publisher. Katherine Krupnik's name was in the upper left return-address corner.

It was the packet of illustrations that Anastasia thought she had put into the mailbox on Chestnut Street at 6:30 that morning.

VALUES

2. *Suppose that by sacrificing one day at the end of your own life — in other words, by dying one day earlier than you otherwise would have — you could save the life of a small child in a Chinese village. Would you do so?*

Well, I guess I would, because if I was old, like maybe ninety, what difference would one day make? Heck, it would probably rain that day anyway. And just think: that Chinese child might grow up to find a cure for some disease, and win the Nobel Prize.

But maybe if that particular day was my birthday or something, probably my family would have planned a big celebration, with a cake with ninety candles or something. So it wouldn't exactly be fair to cancel that day, even if it did save the life of a small child.

Could I make it the day *after* my ninetieth birthday?

3

Anastasia could hardly believe it.

"Sam," she said, "tell Mom I'll be right back, okay? And tell Sleuth I'll be home in a minute, and I'll take him out to play in the yard.

"But right now I have to do a quick errand." Leaving her schoolbooks on the back steps, Anastasia jogged off with her mother's envelope in her hand.

She headed toward the corner of Chestnut and Winchester streets, the site of the mailbox that she had used that morning: the mailbox into which she thought she had deposited her mother's illustrations.

She tried to recreate the moment in her mind. She had stopped near the corner because Sleuth had been nosing around in the shrubbery by the edge of someone's yard. A woman had passed her, walking a tall thin dog on a bright red leather leash, and Anastasia had smiled in response to her cheery greeting, a little embarrassed, she remembered, because Sleuth had chosen that moment to go to the bathroom in the shrubbery.

She remembered that she was glad that the woman had already passed by the time she had knelt to clean up after Sleuth.

She recalled that she had walked on, now holding the warm, bulky plastic bag in her right hand. She had looked around for a trash can, hoping that she could dispose of it; but there were none in sight. There was, however, the mailbox up ahead, on the corner.

She had decided to mail her mother's illustrations and then head home. Sleuth, after all, had fulfilled his mission, so there was no reason to prolong the walk; she could dispose of the blue plastic bag in the trash can back home.

So she had gone to the mailbox, she recalled. Anastasia approached the corner again, now, remembering how hurried she had felt that morning, carrying the unappealing package, and how she had wanted to go home immediately. She had spoken to the dog, she recalled, saying things like, "Good boy, Sleuth, we're heading home as soon as I mail Mom's stuff"; "Good Sleuthie, we'll fix your breakfast in a few minutes"; and he had obediently trotted beside her as if he could understand what she said.

She was very close now. She could see the brick building on the corner. There were more people around now, at (Anastasia checked her watch) 3:20, than there had been at dawn.

In fact, she remembered, there had really been only one person nearby when she mailed (or thought she mailed) the packet. It was the grumpy man. She had been feeling self-conscious because he had seen her scoop, and now he could see the lumpy bundle in her right hand; but she had smiled at the man, who was near the mailbox, and said "Good morning."

He had scowled. He had definitely given her a hostile look — or maybe, actually, he was scowling at the blue bundle in her hand. Sleuth had growled a little, and Anastasia remembered that she didn't blame him, because the grumpy man had invaded the dog's privacy.

But because of the combination of scowl and growl, she had felt uncomfortable — she remembered it clearly now — and had reached to open the mailbox quickly, transferring the dog's leash from one hand to the other, which wasn't easy while holding the mail and also the plastic bag. Then she had tossed it quickly into the mailbox and turned and walked home.

But the "it" she had tossed into the mailbox was not the mail.

She had realized that the instant she saw the bulky envelope in her trash at home. Now, approaching the scene, Anastasia cringed as she actually remembered it quite distinctly. She had felt self-conscious and rushed, with the scowling man nearby, and she had tossed the wrong thing. *Darn it!*

Somehow she hoped that she would not be too late, that perhaps she could undo the error. In the computer program that she used at school, there was an UNDO command. You could get rid of your mistakes if you pressed that command; and you could go back and try again.

Maybe she could UNDO by reaching into the mailbox and down to find the smelly plastic bag still resting there under other people's greeting cards and mortgage payments.

She was still thinking in those terms, fantasizing that she could somehow UNDO unpleasant reality, when she realized that she was there. She was on the corner of Chestnut and Winchester streets, in front of the insurance agency, near the lamppost.

But there was no mailbox in sight. There was no mailbox anywhere. It had been taken away.

Gloomily she trudged home. Hardly thinking about it, she dropped her mother's mail into a mailbox that she spotted on a different corner.

I'll have to call the post office, she thought. *I'll have to ask for the guy in charge, and I'll have to tell him my name, and I'll have to tell him that I'm the one who —*

How on earth can I tell him that?

I'll just be forthright. I'll say, "Hello, my name is Anastasia Krupnik, and I'm very sorry to tell you that because of a foolish mistake, I deposited a bag of —"

No way. I can't do it.

I could say, "Hello, I choose not to tell you my name, I'd prefer to be anonymous, but unfortunately by mistake I put a bag of —"

They could trace the call. I'm sure they could. The post office is part of the government. And I read somewhere that tampering with the mail is a federal offense, so I'm quite sure that they could —

Federal offense. Anastasia's steps slowed when she repeated the phrase to herself. She wasn't entirely certain

33

what it meant; but it sounded grim. Tampering with the mail: she wasn't entirely certain what *that* meant, either.

But maybe she had done it. Maybe, without intending to, she had tampered with the mail.

Maybe she was — or *would be* — in big trouble, if she called the post office.

Maybe she didn't need to call the post office.

If she didn't, how would they ever know who had made the terrible deposit in the mailbox?

She walked on, reached her own house, picked her books up from the back steps, and went inside. The kitchen was empty but it didn't seem deserted. The radio was playing softly, a violin concerto, and a novel by Gail Godwin was lying upside down and open on the table beside her mother's chair. On the refrigerator, a nursery school painting of a rainbow and an airplane dropping bombs was fluttering from its little teapot-shaped magnet. A pot of something tinged with the smell of garlic and herbs was simmering on the stove. From somewhere distant, upstairs, she could hear her mother's voice, and Sam's. After a moment she could hear the tap, tap of dog toenails on the stairs; Sleuth had heard her come home and was coming down to greet her with a big slurpy dog-breath kiss.

For some reason Anastasia suddenly felt like crying. *This is a nice, comfy home,* she thought. *Good people live here. People who make soup and are kind to dogs and small children, who feed their goldfish, who read good literature and listen to classical music. People with Values.*

Of course, her thought continued, *I will call the post office and confess.*

It is the right thing to do.

On the other hand . . .

Why is decision-making so hard? *Why am I such a wishy-washy person?*

Anastasia sighed, decided to think about it all at a later time, and sat down on the kitchen floor to wrestle with her dog instead of her conscience.

"I have to get up early tomorrow," Myron Krupnik said at dinner. "Wake me up, would you, Anastasia, when you go out with the dog? I'll set the alarm but sometimes I go back to sleep by mistake."

Anastasia nodded. "Okay." She poked at her salad. "Why do you have to get up early? I thought you arranged your schedule so that all your classes start at ten."

Her father made a rueful face. "Jury duty," he groaned. "I have to report at eight o'clock."

"No kidding! That sounds like fun!"

But her father shook his head. "No, it's awful. When I filled out the questionnaire they sent me, I tried to think of something that would make me ineligible. But there wasn't anything."

"What would make you ineligible?" Anastasia asked.

"Bad health," her father said.

"You got chicken pox from Sam and you were really sick."

Sam grinned. "Chicken pops," he said, remembering.

"Yes, but I don't have chicken pox *now*," Myron pointed out.

"What else?"

"Oh, let's see, if I were deaf or blind, I'd be ineligible — "

"You have terrible astigmatism," Anastasia reminded him. "I inherited it from you."

"True. But we both can see perfectly well with our glasses."

Mrs. Krupnik looked up from cutting Sam's chicken. "We have a very unreliable car, Myron," she said. "What if you had jury duty and your car wouldn't start?"

But he shook his head. "That wouldn't be an excuse. They'd make you take a cab." He took a bite of chicken. "Nope, I couldn't think of any way to get out of it. There was one question about whether any of your relatives are criminals, and I thought about mentioning my brother George, but — "

"*Myron.*" Mrs. Krupnik scolded him gently, but she was chuckling. "George borrows money and doesn't repay it. That's irritating, not *criminal*. Here, Sam. Eat." She handed Sam his fork.

"What if you lie when you fill out the questionnaire?" Anastasia asked casually.

Her father frowned. "Well, of course I wouldn't *lie*."

"Well, I mean, what if you lied without realizing it? Like, oh, for example, maybe you had a relative who was a criminal but you didn't know it?"

Her dad laughed. "Oh, I suppose they'd catch you somehow. But don't worry about it, sweetie. I didn't lie,

36

and I'm eligible, and I'm on jury duty tomorrow, and
to get up early. So wake me, okay?"

"Duty duty duty kazootie," Sam chanted, and danced
his fork around his mashed potatoes. "*Sam,*" Mrs. Krupnik said firmly, and he grinned and took another bite of his
dinner.

Anastasia sighed and poked at her salad again.

"I think I might use Sleuth as a model," Mrs. Krupnik
announced. They were eating in the kitchen, and the dog,
who was lying in his corner, and who had acquired his
name only that morning, looked up at the sound of it.

"Cool," Anastasia said. "He can be as famous
as — who's that dog in all the books, Sam?"

"Carl," Sam said, without looking up from the road he
was carving through his mashed potatoes. "Carl goes to
daycare. And Carl goes shopping." Sam grinned slyly.
"And Carl goes through mashed potatoes."

"Ha ha," Anastasia said sarcastically to her brother.
Then she turned to her mom. "He's right, though, Mom.
There are a billion Carl books. You could make Sleuth into
a dog detective, or something, and there could be a whole
series. You could get rich. Dad could retire from teaching,
and we could buy a house in, oh, maybe Hawaii, and — "

For a moment, Anastasia had been thinking along the
lines of "and we could move far, far away from the corner
of Chestnut and Winchester." But she reminded herself
that she had decided not to think about that particular
topic.

Her mother laughed. "No, actually, I hadn't planned to
write a book about Sleuth. But remember I told you I have

37

a picture-book text that a publisher sent me, and it happens to have a dog in it? I've done all the preliminary sketches but I didn't fill in the dog because I hadn't decided what kind of dog to use. The author doesn't mention the breed, or even the size or the color. So I thought I might use Sleuth as a model."

The dog, finally, after raising his head at each mention of his name, got up and came over to the table. He sniffed each person's knees as if maybe they had turned edible overnight. Disappointed at the smell of denim, he yawned, went back to his corner, and resumed his disguise as a mop.

Anastasia laughed at the thought of Sleuth posing for her mother, who had been a children's book illustrator for many years, since before Anastasia was born. She had posed for her mom, sometimes, over the years; and so had Sam and their father. Occasionally, when she was in a bookstore or library, she would search for one of those books. There was one called *Lucy-Mousie* about a little girl who had turned into a mouse, and the little girl was actually Anastasia, age six. Anastasia thought the story itself was pretty stupid (and so, in fact, did her mother), but the book was popular, still, and she did enjoy leafing through it to see herself with a long gray tail, little paws, and whiskers poking out below her own horn-rimmed glasses.

There was another book, called *Uncle Dudley and the Dimwits,* for which her father had reluctantly posed as Uncle Dudley. There he was, on almost every page, with his bald head and his beard and his bifocals (but not with his pipe in his mouth; the publisher had told Mrs. Krupnik she couldn't put the pipe in); and on one page, he was wearing his underwear — striped boxers and a T-shirt.

Myron Krupnik, Anastasia's father, had said that if anyone at Harvard, where he taught, ever saw that book and recognized him, he would be ruined as a senior professor of English. But no one ever did.

"This manuscript's a little sad," Katherine Krupnik explained. "It's about a very old woman and her dog."

"Why is it sad?" Anastasia asked.

"Well, because the old woman is clearly very, very old; and so she's looking for a new home for her pet because she knows she won't be around much longer."

Anastasia groaned. "That's gross," she said. "Why do they have to make little kids cry? If I were writing that book, I'd give it a surprise ending, and have the woman live forever and then she'd have to go and get her dog back.

"As a matter of fact," she went on, now that she was warmed up, "if I had written *Little Women,* I'd have penicillin be discovered in time for Beth not to die."

"Great idea!" her father, the English professor, said. "If only Shakespeare had thought of it! Hamlet could die, and then he'd sit up and start laughing and say to the audience, 'Gotcha! Fake rubber sword!' "

Anastasia finished the last of her chicken. "Actually," she said, "that reminds me of something. If you could save the life of one Chinese child by giving up one day of your life, would you do it?" She took her plate to the sink.

"Hong Kong?" her mother asked hesitantly, "or mainland China?"

"I'm not sure," her father said, scrunching his eyebrows. "What if I were in the middle of writing a terrific poem and it needed only one more day's work?

"Or what if I was on jury duty?" he added gloomily.

"Those are really wishy-washy answers," Anastasia said with a sigh.

"Who's Hamlet?" asked Sam, plunging his finger, swordlike, into a mound of potatoes.

Later, sitting at the desk in her bedroom, looking over the answer she had written to question two, Anastasia chewed on a strand of her hair and went on to the third question. At her feet, Sleuth chewed briefly on his paw.

Maybe Sleuth had values to worry about, too, she thought. Probably dogs have moral questions to answer: whether or not to scare a cat, for example, or how violently to bite a burglar.

Question three was another toughie. She wondered what Mr. Francisco would have to say in class tomorrow about the second question, and whether maybe they would have time to talk about the third — assuming, of course, that they were finished with groundhogs.

She glanced over at the clothes folded on the nearby chair. She had laid out the things she planned to wear to school tomorrow. Jeans, of course. She had folded a white blouse — kind of boring — beside the jeans. Then she had added a sweater that she liked a lot; it had a bright yellow and red design.

Briefly she wondered if, for a change, she should wear her hair back in a ponytail tomorrow, and tie something around it. In a little dish on her bureau there was a fat piece of yellow yarn that she had acquired someplace. That would look pretty good with the yellow and red sweater, Anastasia thought.

She walked over to that side of the room, picked up the yarn, held it against her hair, and looked into the mirror. Wasn't there a corny old song that went "And in her hair she wore a yellow ribbon," or something like that?

Yellow ribbon. Yellow ribbon. What was it that someone — just today at school — had said about a yellow ribbon? It was at lunch. It was Meredith. She was talking about —

Oh, no. Anastasia sat down on her bed in dismay as the memory of the conversation came back. Meredith had been talking about the police. About the police that morning. Millions of them — well, okay, four of them — at the corner of Chestnut and Winchester streets. Right by the mailbox — the *former* mailbox, which had now mysteriously disappeared. And an official investigation, probably performed right after the official mailperson from the official mail truck came to officially collect the mail, would have led to the discovery of her gross deposit wrapped in the *New York Times* plastic bag.

The dog ambled over to the bed and sat on the floor by Anastasia's feet, looking up at her lovingly. In his bowl on the bookcase, the goldfish swam languidly in looping arcs.

"Frank," Anastasia whispered in a dispirited, apprehensive voice, "and Sleuthie: stick with me, you guys. I'm in very big trouble with the law."

"*Oooo,*" Frank mouthed silently with his orange glistening lips. "*Oooo.*" Sleuth sneezed.

VALUES

3. *Suppose that by sacrificing one year from your own life expectancy, you could save the life of one American baby. But that baby would grow up to be a violent criminal. Would you do so?*

I guess I would. Because maybe it would do some good stuff before it became a criminal. Or maybe it would be a criminal and then get rehabilitated and do good stuff afterwards, like maybe after it got out of prison it would go to medical school and discover a cure for cancer. I don't think they give the Nobel Prize to former criminals but maybe they might. So I guess I would do it. At least I would if my life expectancy was very long, like if I was going to be ninety or something.

But not if it was going to be a serial killer.

4

"What did you put for number three?" Daphne asked. She and Anastasia were walking together into the school building after meeting on the front steps. Anastasia had taken Sleuth out for his morning walk earlier, but she had chosen a completely different route, one that went nowhere near what she thought of now as the scene of the crime. And she had gone the alternative way to school as well.

Anastasia made a face. "Well, I said *maybe* I would sacrifice a year of my life for a baby criminal. But I don't know, Daph. I don't think he gave us enough information."

Daphne shrugged. "I didn't need any more information. I wouldn't do it. Who cares about criminals? I think they should all get the electric chair."

Anastasia was startled. *"Daphne!"* she said. "That's terrible! You don't believe in the death penalty, do you? How can you? Your father's a minister!"

"Gimme a break," Daphne said sarcastically.

Anastasia sighed as they opened their side-by-side lockers. Poor Daphne; she had developed something of a bad attitude. Anastasia couldn't really blame her. Reverend

Bellingham had a girlfriend who was the soprano soloist in his own church, and they held hands in public, which was about as gross as you could get. And Daphne's mother had announced that all men were pigs; she was in law school now, planning to become a feminist lawyer, and she had stopped using deodorant and always smelled kind of unpleasant. No wonder Daphne was losing her sense of humor.

"I'll see you at lunch, okay?" Anastasia had math first period, and Daphne's schedule was different.

"Can't. I'm being a library aide during lunch period. I'm going to quit eating, anyway."

"How come?"

Daphne giggled. "To get my spirits up. I'm going to get really thin and glamorous. I'm trying to get cheekbones." She sucked her cheeks in and looked at Anastasia.

Anastasia was horrified. She shuddered. "Don't do that, Daph. It makes you look like a skeleton. It gives me the creeps. And it's not healthy to starve yourself."

Daphne laughed, and her sunken cheeks disappeared. "Only kidding," she said. "I have a peanut butter and jelly sandwich in my backpack," she explained. "Mrs. Leonard said I could eat in the library as long as I don't mess up any books."

"Are you coming to Values class?"

Daphne nodded. "I still wouldn't bother giving up any of my own life to save a baby criminal, though. I don't know why you had a hard time answering that question." She grinned and closed the metal door to her locker. "See you later."

Talking to Daphne, thinking about the questions for Mr. Francisco's class, Anastasia had put her own problems out of her mind briefly. It was odd, she thought, how for whole blocks of time she could forget her own terrible secret: that she had not yet confessed to the post office and that they were probably sorting through clues, looking for the lawbreaker.

She was fairly certain that fingerprints wouldn't play a role. Even if her fingerprints were on the blue plastic bag — and they probably were — she didn't think they would be able to match them up. Her fingerprints would not be on file with the FBI, she was quite certain.

And she didn't think they could do anything with DNA. They could get the *dog's* DNA, probably, from the contents of the blue plastic bag; but the dog's DNA wouldn't be on file anyplace, except maybe . . .

At the vet's? But so what? There were a zillion vets in the Boston suburbs, and the post office wouldn't know where to start. They'd look in the same town as the mailbox, and they'd never find him; instead of the town where he lived, Sleuth was a patient of a veterinarian in *Cambridge*, because that's where Anastasia's dad worked. Ha.

And even if by some remote chance they found out who Sleuth was, they could probably never link him to Anastasia Krupnik. If they hauled Sleuth into the police station, she'd say she never saw that dog before in her life. She'd look right at him, into his devoted eyes, and say —

Devoted eyes? That was a joke. Sleuth had so much hair

covering his face that the only way to see his eyes was to conduct an intense search through the underbrush, maybe with a comb.

Anyway, devoted eyes or not, there was no way that Anastasia could pretend that he wasn't her dog. She was a loyal person. If they identified and apprehended Sleuth, she decided, she would have to confess, out of loyalty.

It pleased her, thinking of that. Loyalty was a good quality. It sort of balanced her bad qualities, like wishy-washyness.

But before she could stop herself, she found herself thinking, just for a brief and guilty moment, that she would have been better off if she had gotten a canary instead of a dog.

Anastasia sighed, pushed the whole problem once again to the back of her mind, thought about the math home-work, and entered her first classroom of the day.

It was early afternoon. Mr. Francisco came into the room and Anastasia opened her notebook and turned to the Values questions.

"So, guys," Mr. Francisco said to the class, "now that we've buried the groundhog, what're we going to do about these babies? Gonna sacrifice a few days of your own lives?"

He sat on the desk at the front of the room, and Anastasia thought again about what an attractive man Mr. Francisco was. Anastasia didn't ordinarily notice what clothes men wore. She couldn't remember what her father had been wearing at breakfast that morning, even though he had probably been dressed in a very dignified fashion, maybe even with a necktie, for jury duty.

But for some reason she noticed that Mr. Francisco was wearing a plaid shirt, which she had seen in the L.L. Bean catalog, with an oatmeal-colored crewneck sweater over it.

She sighed. Mr. Francisco never seemed to notice her very much. He concentrated his attention on the people who had strong opinions. He liked to provoke them into arguments. Then, before they knew what had happened, he had turned the whole argument around so that their opinions had changed.

Her own opinions could never change, she thought glumly, because she didn't have opinions to begin with.

As usual, her classmates were digressing. They were talking about criminal behavior, and whether you could identify it early. The discussion caught Anastasia's attention. After all, she herself now fell into the category of criminal, even though nobody knew it yet. Most of the boys were raising their hands and telling about murderers they had read about, or had seen interviewed on TV.

"They're always loners," someone said. "The newspaper always says, 'Neighbors described him as a loner.'"

Anastasia wondered if neighbors would describe her as a loner. Probably not. They would describe her as someone who was always with either three girlfriends, a small brother, or a leashed dog who resembled a mop.

"They never look like murderers," Ben Barstow said

with authority, as if he were a college professor. "They look like accountants. They always wear weird shoes."

Anastasia gulped. She *did* look like an accountant. She was sure of it. She wore big round horn-rimmed glasses, exactly like the guys — the accountants — from Price Waterhouse who brought out the names of the Oscar winners at the Academy Awards ceremonies.

She glanced down at her shoes. Hiking boots. Were they weird? Anastasia didn't think so.

"Yeah, but even if they don't look like murderers, you can *tell!*" Steve Harvey insisted. "My mom says you can tell. Like that guy in the movie, Hannibal Lecter? You could tell by how weird he acted."

Steve's mom — the Harveys were neighbors of the Krupniks — was a prosecuting attorney, so she knew lots of criminals. She was always going to crime scenes and stuff, and she had to conduct interviews in prisons and police stations. It had always seemed to Anastasia that Mrs. Harvey had a very scary but exciting job.

Mr. Francisco began to direct the discussion away from criminal identification, back to the original question and the problem of how to make decisions on difficult issues.

Anastasia's mind wandered again. She wondered if Mrs. Harvey would be the one to prosecute her when she was caught. *If* she were caught.

She wondered if her father would be a member of the jury. Probably not. Probably it would disqualify him, having his daughter be the criminal.

The accused *criminal,* Anastasia reminded herself. Her

parents had often talked about how people in America were innocent until they were proven guilty.

She wondered if maybe she ought to confess, and plea-bargain, or should she proclaim her innocence — which would involve lying, something Anastasia did not ordinarily do — or maybe even go for an insanity defense?

It *had* been, she thought, a completely insane thing to do. Maybe a psychiatrist would testify on her behalf.

"The defendant has been seriously disturbed since early adolescence," the psychiatrist would testify, looking at his notes on the witness stand. "She had an unnatural relationship with a goldfish dating back to fourth grade."

The jury would gaze at her with loathing.

"Anastasia?" Mr. Francisco's voice called her back from her thoughts. She looked up. He was still sitting on the desk top, swinging his legs. (He wore loafers, she noticed, comfortable-looking, tastefully scuffed loafers.) "What did you decide?"

Anastasia read her answer to question three, the question about sacrificing some of your own life for the sake of a future criminal, aloud. "It's a wishy-washy answer, isn't it?" she asked Mr. Francisco.

"Hey, it was a tough question. Isn't that right, class? These decisions aren't easy. We always want to say, 'But what if . . .?'

"Think about the what ifs while you take a look at the next two questions for Monday's class, guys. And have a good weekend, okay?"

❖   ❖   ❖

Anastasia walked partway home with her three best friends, as usual. One by one they separated as they came to their respective streets. Daphne Bellingham headed off first, toward the apartment building where she lived with her mother.

"See ya," she said, at her corner. "I'll call you all tonight."

"What are you going to do this weekend?" Meredith Halberg asked her. "Should we all get together? We could rent a movie or something."

"Okay," Daphne said. "I have to spend Sunday with my dad, but I could come over tomorrow. In the afternoon or evening, okay? I'm going to spend the morning working on my looks."

"Your looks?" Sonja asked, puzzled. "What's wrong with your looks? You're one of the best-looking girls in the eighth grade. Everybody says so."

"Right," Anastasia and Meredith both agreed, nodding. Daphne made a face.

"You're not really going to starve yourself into cheek-bones, are you?" Anastasia asked suspiciously.

"No," Daphne explained. "Actually, I'm just working on my wardrobe. My mom said I could have all of her feminine clothes. She's only going to wear — what did she call it? — *genderless* clothing from now on. She's changing her style, so I get a whole lot of new clothes. Everything that has a ruffle or a ribbon or a piece of lace."

"How can you change your style of looks?" Anastasia asked, mystified. "You look like what you look like. I look like an owl, for example. No matter what I do to change it,

I'll always look like an owl. I've resigned myself to that."

Sonja nodded in assent. "I'll always look like a porpoise," she said, sighing. "My whole family looks like porpoises. I think we're called a pod."

Meredith frowned. "How come you all know what you look like and I don't?"

The other three all gazed at Mer for a moment. She was tall and thin, a very pale blonde with light blue eyes.

"You look like an Afghan hound," Anastasia said, finally. "I'll show you a picture in my dog book. Why don't you all come over to my house tomorrow night? I told my parents I'd baby-sit for Sam; they're going to the theater."

"Can we rent a movie? You have a VCR, don't you?" Daphne asked.

"Sure. Hey, I have an idea. We can rent a movie my dad knows about; he said it's a good one. It's called *Sleuth,* same as my dog."

They waved to Daphne. At the next corner, Sonja said good-bye and headed to the sprawling house where her large family lived and where, in a separate wing, her father had his medical office; then Meredith turned toward her own brick house in the block before Anastasia's.

Anastasia walked on alone to her own house. It was certainly not the most elegant house on the street, but it was a house that Anastasia loved, with its Victorian turret that housed her third-floor bedroom, its large yard and porches, and the glassed-in room on the side which was her mother's studio. She thought about how pleasant it would be to have her friends over for the evening tomorrow night. There was some Paul Newman popcorn in the cupboard, she remembered, and maybe she could make some cookies in the morning, and let Sam help.

Of course, it meant that she would have to postpone her other plans a little. She had almost convinced herself to call the post office this afternoon and confess.

But Mr. Francisco had been correct. If you started thinking about the "But what ifs," it all became hopelessly complicated.

For example, what if she confessed, and she had already rented the movie, and they wouldn't let her take it back before she went off to jail? Well, of course her father would probably return it for her, but she had asked him lots of other times to return movies for her, and he had always been grouchy about doing it.

And what if after she confessed, her picture was in the newspaper, and it would be one of those terrible mug shots that they take at the police station, maybe they would even use the profile one, and Anastasia had a *terrible* profile, even on a not-too-bad-hair day, and no lawyer would want to represent someone who looked like that, not even Alan Dershowitz, even though her dad had met him at a party in Cambridge once?

Who would feed Frank Goldfish while she served her sentence?

And what about Sleuth? What if her parents weren't willing to walk Sleuth while she was imprisoned, even though it would probably be a fairly short prison term, because after all, it was only tampering with the mail, not mass murder or anything? What would happen to Sleuthie then?

53

What if she got a terrible cellmate? Anastasia didn't even like summer camp because there was no privacy. She couldn't *imagine* being shut up in a tiny cell with some other person (she supposed it would be a female, at least) who maybe sleepwalked or, even worse, *smoked?*

To confess or not to confess. To confess today or wait till after the weekend.

I am not going to be wishy-washy about this, Anastasia decided. *I have absolutely come to a decision. I am a person with values, and confessing is the right thing to do. It's the honorable thing. I will confess.*

I just won't confess yet.

VALUES

4. *Suppose that you happened to see a stranger shoplifting in one of your favorite stores. Would you report it to the store manager?*

Well, I guess I would report it. Because the prices of things in stores go up if there is a lot of shoplifting, since the store has to make up for the loss of income. My favorite store is Strawberries, where I buy CD's, and they are already too expensive. So I would do my part to put a halt to shoplifting.

Also, of course, stealing is wrong, and I would report it for that reason, too.

On the other hand, though, I wouldn't want the person to know I reported them, because what if they were a hardened criminal or something, and would take revenge on me? If they were just shoplifting a CD, it wouldn't be worth it to risk my life.

If they were shoplifting a whole stereo system, then maybe it would be worth it. But what if they took revenge on my whole family? Even my little brother?

5

"Sit, Sleuth. Now *stay*." Anastasia could hear her mother's voice from the studio where Katherine Krupnik worked. She walked down the hall, through the dining room, and opened the door that was the entrance to the huge, octagonal, multiwindowed room attached to the side of their big house.

She remembered that when they had looked at the house with a real estate agent before they bought it the previous year, the woman had opened this door and said, "You could close it off to conserve heat. Or, in fact, you could even have this room torn down. It does stick out rather awkwardly from the side of the house . . ."

Anastasia and her parents had looked at each other that day more than a year ago as if they shared a secret, and of course they did: the secret was that the real estate lady was a complete idiot, and that they were going to buy this house despite her.

Now she looked at her mother, who was standing at her big tilted drawing table. In a corner, Sam was quietly playing with his Lego set.

Sleuth, responding perfectly to the command Anastasia had heard her mother give, was sitting alertly in the middle of the room. He was a very obedient dog. The Krupniks had been lucky. Whoever had owned Sleuth before, even though they had given him a dumb name like Louie, had clearly spent some time training him. He never chewed anything except his toys; he walked happily on a leash, without pulling; he came when you called him; and now he was behaving exactly like a perfect model should. He sat motionless, though his tail wagged when Anastasia entered the room.

"Now look sorrowful," Mrs. Krupnik said. She frowned and made some strokes on the paper with her pencil. "Look sad, please, Sleuthie."

Anastasia laughed aloud and her mother looked up. "Oh, hi, sweetie," she said. "I'm having a terrible time with the dog." She turned to the dog, who hadn't moved. "Take a short break, Sleuth," she told him. He stood up and came over to welcome Anastasia, who scratched his shaggy head.

"How come? It looked like he was a better model than I am. I always have to scratch my nose."

"Oh, he's great at sitting still," her mother explained. "But — well, here. I'll explain the plot of this book to you."

"You did already. The old woman is going to die so she has to find a home for her pet. It's guaranteed to give nightmares to every toddler in America. I would have hated it when I was little. Sam will hate it."

Sam looked up from the large red and white tower he was building. "I do," he said cheerfully. "I hate it."

"No, no," Mrs. Krupnik went on. "It's not that bad, actually. It doesn't say she's dying. It says she's getting old and can't take proper care of the dog . . . his name is; oh, what is his name? Let me think; oh, his name is Toby . . . and so she starts looking for a happy home. The title, by the way, is *Want a Dog?*

"Anyway, first she takes him to the home of a TV comedian. See, I've done some sketches. These are copies, actually. I mailed the originals to the publisher yesterday. As a matter of fact, you mailed them for me. Thank you."

Anastasia managed a weak smile.

She looked over her mother's shoulder at the rough sketches of a man wearing a bad toupee and a fake smile. Around him, family members were doubled up, laughing. It was a pretty funny drawing, Anastasia thought.

"The comedian is telling these terrible jokes: 'Who was that lady I saw you with last night?' — that kind of thing.

"And the dog is supposed to look so miserable that the old lady says 'Thank you' politely to the comedian's family and takes the dog away."

Anastasia looked with interest at a sketch of the old lady leaving the house. She was holding a leash, but at the end of it was a blank space because the dog hadn't been sketched in yet. In the background, the comedian was still gesturing and grinning and holding a fake microphone.

"Then she takes him to the home of a clown."

Anastasia chuckled and looked at the sketches of a frenzied clown with a big greasepaint smile. He was riding a unicycle and juggling some balls. In the front of the scene was a blank space where obviously the dog would be.

58

"I get it," Anastasia said. "He's going to look miserable here, too."

"Right. She takes him to all these wildly cheerful places, but he gets sadder and sadder. So eventually she has to take him back home. See?" Mrs. Krupnik shuffled through the papers and found one that showed the old woman from the back, walking dejectedly toward her little house, with the leash coming from her hand, and a blank space where the dejected dog would be.

"But how will it end?" Anastasia asked.

"Here." Mrs. Krupnik handed her a sketch of a little boy walking past the house. The boy's head was down. His shoulders were slumped, and from one hand he was dragging a string with a pathetic-looking wooden toy attached to it.

"Oh, I get it!" Anastasia said. "That blank place in the window is where the dog will be looking out."

"Right. With his head up and his tail wagging."

"And the old lady will call through the window and say — "

"*Want a Dog?*"

At Anastasia's feet, Sleuthie wagged his tail agreeably.

"You're right, Mom. I don't hate it. It's cute, actually. But why are you having a problem with Sleuth?"

"Well, he sits, and he stays, and he lies down when I tell him to, and he stays in any position that I want him in. But his expression never changes. I can't seem to get him to look sad or miserable, and I suspect that when I get to that last picture, when he's in the window, even if I can get him to wag his tail, which I probably can, he still won't look exuberant and happy. He doesn't seem to change his facial expression at all."

"Mom," Anastasia pointed out, surprised that her mother hadn't noticed. "Sleuth doesn't *have* a face. How can he have a facial expression when he has no face?"

Her mother stared at Sleuth. From his corner, Sam, too, looked over at Sleuth.

Sleuth looked back at them. Or at least they assumed that he was looking back at them. All they could see was hair, with a black nose poking out of it.

"Anastasia, you're absolutely right. It's because you can't see his eyes. In order to have a facial expression, you have to have eyes!" Mrs. Krupnik leaned down and held Sleuth's hair up to expose his eyes. There they were: big and brown and long-lashed and adoring. Suddenly Sleuth had a facial expression. But when she dropped the handful of hair, he became expressionless again.

"Well, I'll have to think about this. I don't want to have to hire a dog model." Mrs. Krupnik tapped her pencil thoughtfully against the tabletop. "Maybe in the meantime I'll have a cup of coffee. It's probably time to start dinner, anyway. How was school?"

Anastasia followed her mother down the hall toward the kitchen. Behind them came Sam, with his arms full of Legos, which were falling piece by piece on the floor behind him; and then Sleuth, who sniffed, examined, and then padded his way past the red and white bits of plastic.

"School was okay. Can I have Daphne, Sonja, and Meredith over tomorrow night while I'm baby-sitting? And rent a movie?"

"May," her mother corrected automatically.

"I meant 'May I,' " Anastasia replied.

"Don't say baby-sitting," Sam commanded. It was a word that he despised.

"Sorry, Sam. I forgot. I meant 'boy-sitting.' "

Mrs. Krupnik laughed and poured herself some coffee from the pot on the stove. "Sure, I guess so, if their parents don't mind. Dad and I will be back around eleven, and we could drive them all home then."

"Could we rent *Sleuth,* do you think?"

At the sound of his name, the dog became alert, with his ears up and his tail wagging vigorously.

"Sure," her mother said. "But feed him first," she added, laughing.

"How was jury duty, Dad?" Anastasia asked when her father came home. She could almost guess the answer, because he looked exhausted and miserable.

He grunted. Then he undid his necktie, took it off, and loosened the collar of his shirt. He sat down, with his shoulders slumped, at the kitchen table.

Mrs. Krupnik, who'd been preparing dinner, brought him a cup of coffee. Then, while he sipped, she stood behind him and massaged his shoulders and neck. Sleuth, who seemed to sense that the master of the house was unhappy, came over and lay at his feet, snuggling between Myron Krupnik's two size-twelve shoes.

Finally, after he had relaxed for a minute, Anastasia's dad answered her question.

"It was horrible," he said flatly.

61

"How come? I thought it would be fun."

He sighed. "Never use the word 'fun' to describe the judicial process," he told her. "It is very, very serious. There was not one minute of *fun* all day."

"Yeah," Anastasia said, "I guess I was thinking of *Night Court* on TV."

"All of us gathered there at eight this morning," Mr. Krupnik explained, "and we waited around, and a judge came in and explained the whole thing to us, how it would work, and then we waited around again. Every now and then they would come in and collect one group of people — we all had numbers — and they would take that group away to ask them some questions and figure out if they would actually serve on a jury.

"There are lots of different trials going on at the same time," he explained. Anastasia nodded.

"So I sat and sat and sat, and read the *New York Times* over and over. I even read all the small print: what restaurants were closed this week for health violations, who had a baby."

"Who had a baby?" asked Sam, with interest.

Myron Krupnik thought. He rubbed his beard. Finally he said, "Heidi and Michael Kooperman welcome Alisa Michelle, beautiful baby sister for Matthew and Jared."

Anastasia stared at him. "You made that up, didn't you, Dad?"

He shook his head sadly. "No."

"Poor Myron," Katherine Krupnik said, and poured him a little more coffee.

"Anyway, finally they called my number, and I went into

a courtroom with a group, and it was just like on TV, with a judge up there on the bench. And he described the case and started asking us questions."

"Like what?"

"Well, he read us a list of all the lawyers and all the witnesses, and he asked if we knew any of them."

"Did you? You and Mom know a lot of lawyers."

"Nope. I was hoping I would, because then I would have been excused. Some of the jurors got to leave at that point. But I didn't recognize a single name."

"What happened then?"

"Well, then he called our numbers, and we had to go sit in the jury box, and the trial started."

"Just like on TV?"

"Right. But the worst thing was, the judge looked through the list of jurors. He had all those questionnaires we'd filled out. And he appointed *me* foreman. I had to switch seats with someone and sit in the front seat."

"Why did he choose you?"

"Beats me."

"I bet you were the only guy with a beard."

"Well, I was, as a matter of fact."

"Was it fun — I mean, interesting — after that, when the trial started? Did the defendant sit there glaring at you with glittering piggy eyes?" Anastasia was very curious.

"Well, the defendant *looked* at us. I wouldn't call it glaring. And it was interesting at first. The lawyers each made opening statements — "

"Just like on TV."

"Right. Then they started with witnesses."

63

"Just like — "

"Right. And I listened carefully, because I knew how important it was."

"You're always a very good listener, Myron," Mrs. Krupnik said from the sink, where she was washing lettuce.

"And after the prosecution had presented their witnesses — it didn't take very long, just a couple of hours — I was feeling pretty good about everything. It was clear the accused person was guilty. Then we stopped for lunch. We went in a jury room, and they brought us sandwiches."

"Did you talk about the guilty person while you had lunch?"

"No, we weren't allowed to. We talked about football, mostly."

"Then what? You went back to court, and said 'Guilty'?"

Anastasia's father groaned. "No, we went back in the courtroom, and the defense presented their witnesses."

"Did anybody cry on the witness stand?" Anastasia asked. "Sometimes they do on TV."

"No. Nobody cried. I almost did, though."

Anastasia giggled. "Why?"

"Because when I listened to the defense witnesses, I became convinced that the defendant was innocent."

"But you just said — "

"Right."

"Oh, dear," Mrs. Krupnik said. She came over and sat down. "What did you do?"

"Well, I kept listening carefully. And after all the witnesses had testified, there were closing arguments. And when I listened to them, first I thought: *Guilty.*

"Then I thought: *Not guilty.*

"Finally we went into the jury room and we had to come up with a verdict."

Anastasia nodded. "Just like on — "

"Right. And there we sat. Half of the people said, 'Absolutely guilty, no question.' And the other half said, 'Absolutely innocent, no question.' And they kept arguing and looking at *me,* because I was the foreman."

"What did you say?"

Her father sighed loudly. "I was wishy-washy," he confessed. "I said I couldn't make up my mind."

"*Just like me!*" Anastasia announced. "I know just what you feel like."

"But what did you do, Myron?"

"We all argued a lot, and it was getting late. People wanted to go home. One woman had a baby-sitter who had to leave at six. Somebody else had a bad headache. Finally, because we couldn't decide, we said to each other that there must be a reasonable doubt. So we decided on a verdict of not guilty. We went back to the courtroom and I announced that to the judge."

"Just — "

"Right, Anastasia. Exactly like on TV. The defendant shook hands with the lawyer and left. And we all left, too.

"You know what? I think that was one of the hardest things I've ever done in my life. Do I have time to listen to Brahms's Double Concerto before dinner, Katherine?"

"Sure," she said. "I'll call you when it's ready."

Anastasia followed her father down the hall toward the study. "Don't you feel good, though, Dad? Because after all, if it weren't for you, an innocent man might have been convicted and sentenced to a life behind bars, and the real murderer would have gone free. Even though you *suffered*, Dad, it was a monumentally important thing to have done."

Myron Krupnik searched through the B's in his CD collection, took out the Brahms concerto, inserted it into the stereo, and turned it on. He sank down onto the couch and stretched his long legs, listening to the first surging notes of the violin.

"And *now*, Dad," Anastasia went on, "they'll find the real killer, and eventually justice will be done! All because of your courage in holding out for a Not Guilty verdict!"

He chuckled. "Sweetie," he said to her, "it sounds like a lot of drama, but in all honesty it wasn't a federal case or anything. The defendant was an eighteen-year-old girl accused of driving without a license."

Later that evening, feeding her fish, Anastasia said nervously, "Frank, this is a tough time coming up, and I want you to be patient with me if I don't pay a whole lot of light-hearted attention to you the way I used to. I may have to be preparing for a trial soon."

She sat down at her desk and read question five with a feeling of misery and hopelessness.

It was Anastasia's very favorite kind of night. Outside, it was raining heavily and the wind was blowing. Water spattered the windowpanes and tree branches brushed and tapped the side of the house.

But inside, in the study, a fire was glowing and crackling in the fireplace. There was a huge bowl of Paul Newman popcorn and four cans of Pepsi on the coffee table. The dog was curled up, looking like a mop, on the floor; occasionally he twitched or stirred as if he might be chasing a squirrel in his doggy dreams. Anastasia and her three best friends, silent except for an occasional munch or sip, were watching Laurence Olivier and Michael Caine pretend to be civilized and witty, while the two were actually scaring each other to death in *Sleuth*.

Upstairs, wearing his Batman pajamas, Sam was sound asleep.

"Can you put it on pause?" Meredith asked. "I have to go to the bathroom."

Anastasia stopped the film, and they waited while Meredith went down the hall to the small half-bath near the entrance to the house. Sonja stood up, pushed the draperies aside, and looked out at the rain. "That looks like a haunted house next door," she said. "It's all dark."

Anastasia laughed. "That's Mrs. Stein's house," she said. "She goes to bed early. She's really old. When we first moved in here, Sam thought she was a witch, like in a Halloween story, because her hair was all messy and she has a kind of pointy nose. But she's really nice. Sometimes she baby-sits for Sam if I can't."

She looked through the window where Sonja was standing. "See over there?" She pointed. "That great big house

67

down the street with the fence around the yard? That's where Steve Harvey lives."

"No kidding. Is he rich?"

Anastasia shrugged. "I guess so. His dad's a sports-caster, remember? And his mom's a lawyer."

"Who's rich?" Meredith asked, coming back into the study.

"Steve Harvey. That's his house," Anastasia explained, pointing it out again.

Daphne, who had been leafing through a magazine, looked up from the couch where she was sprawled. "Do you think after my mom finishes law school she'll get rich? I'm sick of living in a crummy apartment."

"Probably. But you'll be old by then," Meredith pointed out cheerfully. "Hey, I have an idea! How about if we call up Steve Harvey anonymously?"

Anastasia made a face. "That's such an adolescent thing to do, Mer. I did that when I was in sixth grade."

"Yeah, you're right," Meredith acknowledged. "It was a dumb idea. You really have values, Anastasia. Did you answer question four yet, about the shoplifter?"

"Yeah, I have it right here." Anastasia went to her father's desk, where she had been working on her home-work. "All of my answers are actually *non*-answers," she explained miserably. "I can't ever make up my mind. Listen to this." She read her answer to the shoplifter question aloud.

"Heck, I thought that one was easy," Daphne said. "I'd turn him in. I'd call the cops on him."

Sonja looked startled. "I thought it was easy, too," she said, "but I said the opposite. I'd look the other way. It's his problem, not mine."

"Not me," Meredith said. "I agree with Daphne. Call the cops. No question."

Anastasia sighed and folded her paper again. "I can't figure out why everything is so easy for everyone else but me. Don't you think about the what ifs? What if the shoplifter is a woman?"

"Who cares? I'd report her. It would be sexist not to," Daphne said firmly.

Meredith agreed. "Yeah, I would, too," she said.

Anastasia was thinking. "What if," she said finally, "the shoplifter is a friend of yours? That's the next question. We're supposed to do two over the weekend," she reminded them.

"A close friend?" asked Daphne. "I haven't looked at question five yet."

Anastasia nodded. "Your very best friend," she said solemnly. "Wouldn't you be indecisive *then*?"

All four girls fell silent. Outside, the rain pelted the windows.

"I don't think it would be a problem," Sonja ventured after a moment's thought.

Anastasia heard the tentative quality in her reply. "Ha!" she said. "See? *Then* you'd be wishy-washy like me, I bet anything. You wouldn't be able to make up your mind! Right?"

But Sonja shook her head firmly. "No," she said. "That's

why you guys are my best friends. Because you all have values the same as mine. None of you would ever shoplift, would you?"

"No." Daphne, Meredith, and Anastasia all agreed that they wouldn't.

"So," Sonja pointed out. "It's easy. I just wouldn't *have* friends who would break the law."

"I wouldn't either," Meredith agreed cheerfully.

"Me neither," Daphne said, picking up a magazine. After a moment's silence, Anastasia said, "Yeah. Right." She went to the VCR and pushed play. On the screen, Laurence Olivier appeared, smiling his sophisticated, somewhat sinister smile.

VALUES

5. *Suppose you happened to see a good friend shoplifting. Would you report it to the store manager?*

Well, I guess I would. No, wait. I think I'd tell the friend first that I'd seen her. I'd ask her to put the stuff back, and if she did, I wouldn't tell. And I think she would put it back. Partly because she'd be afraid I'd report her. But partly because I'd remind her that stealing is wrong.

If she didn't put it back, then I guess maybe I'd report it. Because in the long run it would be the best thing for her, to be punished. Not jail or anything, though. Maybe *some* criminals deserve to go to jail, but I think it's possible for somebody to do a criminal act without being a real criminal. Maybe they would just be someone who made a really dumb mistake that happened to be a federal offense.

I don't think that person, the one who just made a dumb mistake and who might happen to be your good friend, should have to have a trial or anything. Maybe that person has her whole life in front of her.

6

Question five really got to her. Anastasia thought about it a lot over the remainder of the weekend. She thought about it even after she had finished writing her response to it.

Anastasia knew a lot of kids who shoplifted. Some of them bragged about it. But she thought they were losers, the same way she thought that kids who smoked were losers.

Yet even though she knew who they were, and thought they were losers, she had not reported them to anyone.

She *could* have. She could have gone to, say, Mrs. Johnson, the guidance counselor; or to Mr. Francisco — even better, since he was so cool and so easy to talk to — and she could have said, "You know that baseball cap that Ben Barstow always wears? I happen to know that he stole it from a store in Copley Place. He was telling everybody about how he just put it on and walked out of the store."

She could have, but she hadn't. And she knew she wasn't going to.

She reread her answer, wondering if she had lied without intending to. She had not told Ben that she knew about his shoplifting; why should she, when he had bragged about it already? But she had not reported him, either.

Anastasia read the question again at the same time, trying to apply it to Ben Barstow. She felt relieved. It *wasn't* a lie, because the question had specifically said "a good friend."

Ben Barstow was not a good friend. She didn't even *like* Ben Barstow much. Not many kids did. They called him Ben Barstool.

She read question four again, just to see whether perhaps Ben Barstow fit into that one. But no. Question four definitely said "a stranger."

Still, she realized, thinking about it some more, the whole thing was making her a little uncomfortable. She wondered uneasily what her own friends would do if they knew that she was a lawbreaker.

Early Sunday morning, Anastasia got up grudgingly when the dog, who had learned to nudge open the door to the room where he slept, padded up the stairs to her bedroom on the third floor and stood impatiently beside her bed, touching her face affectionately with his damp nose.

"I wish you'd learn that weekends are a time of *rest*, Sleuth," she muttered as she pulled her sweatpants on and looked around in the dim dawn light for a shirt. "I don't mind school mornings because I have to get up anyway, but couldn't you sleep late on Saturdays and Sundays, like most people?"

The dog, sitting on the floor beside her bed, listened to her voice with interest as he watched her dress. He cocked his head as if he were trying to think of an answer.

Anastasia read his mind and sighed. "I know," she said, tugging on her socks, "you're not a person, you're a dog."

His tail thumped against the floor.

She tied her sneakers and reached for her glasses on the table beside her bed. No need, she had decided, to comb her hair for dog-walking. She never saw anybody who mattered.

Alert and attentive, Sleuth stood and headed for the stairs. He knew by now that Anastasia's glasses were the signal. When she put her glasses on, she was ready to take him out. Eagerly he led her down two flights of stairs to the front hall, and went to the table where his leash was kept in a drawer. He wiggled with excitement while she clipped it to his collar. Then he waited while she picked up her father's thick Sunday *New York Times* from the front steps, took it out of its plastic bag, and wadded the bag into her pocket.

"Okay, Sleuth, *heel*," Anastasia said, as she did every morning. Happily letting her think that she was in charge, he pranced by her side and surveyed the neighborhood to be sure it hadn't undergone any changes during the night. He sniffed one bush, decided against it, chose another and lifted his leg briefly, then looked intently for a long time at an empty, crumpled Marlboro package in the gutter.

"Don't even think about sniffing that, Sleuth," Anastasia said. "It'll give you cancer." Disdainfully she picked it up between her thumb and first finger and put it into the plastic bag. She didn't want it messing up the street in front of her house, and figured it deserved to be in a dog-poop bag which would end up . . . *in the trash can,* she reminded herself, as she now did every morning. She never took mail with her now on her morning walk. One thing about making a really awful mistake, Anastasia realized, was that you never made it a second time.

She had never, in fact, taken the route of the first morning again. Today, Sunday, she decided that she would.

Criminal Returns to Scene, she said to herself as she made the turn that would take her toward the corner of Chestnut and Winchester. It was a little like getting back on a horse after having been thrown: a scary but necessary thing to do.

Not that Anastasia had ever in her life been thrown from a horse, or even ridden a horse. Many of her friends — especially Meredith, who went to riding camp every summer — were horse-crazy. Meredith always spent half the month of September talking about Blaze, or Golden Girl, or whatever horse had been her favorite that summer. Meredith owned jodhpurs and jodhpur boots and a riding helmet and sometimes was very boring when talking about horse shows.

Anastasia didn't have any interest in horses. But she did remember that if a horse threw you off, you were sup-posed to get up, dust off your jodhpurs, and climb right back on. If you didn't, fear had gotten the better of you, and so had the horse.

She decided that the same thing applied to the corner of

75

Chestnut and Winchester streets. If she couldn't bring herself to walk past it again, fear would have conquered her. So she jerked at the leash when Sleuth started to turn right at the usual place, and turned left instead. She hoped that the corner would look the way it had in her past life, in her precriminal existence, with a fat blue mailbox sitting there, waiting to be filled by innocent letter-writers and bill-payers.

She took a deep breath, building her own self-confidence, and said to the dog, "See, Sleuth? I'm going back to the scene. It hasn't gotten the best of me."

Sleuth, hearing her voice, looked up at her with his shaggy non-face. He didn't care which way they went, as long as there were bushes to inspect, lampposts to sprinkle, dead leaves to probe suspiciously with his nose and paws, and dog scents to analyze.

"Maybe someday," Anastasia told him as they approached the corner, "this will feel like a comfortable, familiar spot to me. Maybe I'll actually mail a letter here again."

But when they arrived at the spot, the mailbox was still missing. There were scars in the sidewalk where it had been removed.

"You know a weird thing?" Anastasia said to Sonja and Meredith in the school cafeteria on Monday. The three of them were eating lunch together. Daphne was working in the library again.

"What?" Sonja asked, poking through the salad on her plastic plate, looking for some lettuce that didn't have rust-colored stains on its edges. "What's weird? Aside from this salad, I mean."

"The mailbox on the corner of Chestnut and Winchester streets is gone." Anastasia said it very casually, and took a bite of her grilled cheese sandwich.

"Why is that weird? Who cares about mailboxes?" Meredith asked. "You know what *I* think is weird? Our new gym teacher. I wish Ms. Willoughby hadn't left."

Anastasia wished that too, because she had been very fond of Ms. Willoughby. But she didn't want to talk about gym teachers. "It isn't that I care about mailboxes particularly," she explained. "But I just think it's strange, that it would be on that corner for about a thousand years, and then suddenly it isn't."

Sonja gave up on her salad and started investigating her vegetable soup with a spoon. "You mean that same corner where the police were last week?"

Anastasia nodded.

"Probably there was a car accident, and somebody bashed into that mailbox, and so they had to throw it away," Sonja suggested. She stirred until a bit of carrot floated to the surface, and then finally took a bite of soup. "Yuck," she said, making a face. "I hate this lunch."

Anastasia brightened. She hadn't thought of that possibility. "Yeah! Maybe a car hit it and that's why the police were there, and probably the mailbox got absolutely flattened, and they had to take it to the dump!"

That's it! Anastasia thought. *That's what happened! They took the whole thing to the dump after a car hit it, and so no one ever found out what I did!* It felt as if a weight had been lifted.

"Well, they couldn't just take it to the dump, even if it was flat," Meredith pointed out.

"Why not?"

"Because first they'd have to pry it open and get the contents out. They can't just throw away *mail*."

"The *police* could," Anastasia insisted. "The police can do just about anything they want."

"Nope," Sonja said. "Maybe our town police can do pretty much anything in this town. But mailboxes belong to the government. If the police took mail to the dump, it would be a federal offense. They'd go to some federal prison."

"What *is* a federal prison?" Anastasia asked. She really didn't understand about federal offenses, even though they sounded very grave.

Sonja shrugged. "I don't know exactly. But it's not like regular jail or anything. It's where serious criminals go, like politicians who take bribes. And people who tamper with the mail."

"I don't understand *tampering* exactly," Anastasia confessed nervously. The weight that had been lifted was back, heavier than ever.

"It means messing with," Meredith said. "Like Sonja is right now tampering with that soup. A minute ago Sonja tampered with her salad."

Sonja and Meredith laughed. They both seemed awfully lighthearted, Anastasia thought gloomily. They wouldn't be so all-fired *merry* if they knew that they were having lunch with someone who had tampered with mail. Who had *messed with* mail in about the messiest way possible.

Daphne appeared suddenly. She dropped her books on the table and flopped into an empty chair beside Sonja. "There wasn't anybody in the library," she announced, "and all the books were shelved. So I spent my time reading about transvestism."

"Want my soup? I hate it," Sonja asked her.

Daphne glanced at it and shook her head.

"She tampered with it already," Meredith said, giggling.

"Reading about *what?*" Anastasia asked.

"Transvestism," Daphne repeated. "That's when people are compelled to wear clothes of the opposite sex. It's not curable, as far as they know."

Anastasia frowned. "Why would you want to cure it?" she asked. "I wear my dad's shirts a lot. But I wouldn't exactly say I'm *compelled,*" she added.

Sonja pinched a bit of her sweater between two fingers and held it out. "See this? It's my brother's. He got it for his birthday and he said it sucked. So my mom said I could have it. I don't want to be cured. I really like this sweater."

Daphne sighed. "I was looking it up because of my mother. My mother bought a *necktie.*"

Nobody said anything. Anastasia felt herself begin to laugh.

"What's so funny?" Daphne asked gloomily.

"Nothing. I'm sorry," Anastasia said. "But I wouldn't

worry about it, Daph. Neckties are cool. Sunday's *New York Times* magazine had a whole fashion section, and a lot of models were wearing neckties."

"Females?"

"Yeah. Females. Really."

Daphne leaned over and began picking at the leftovers on her friends' trays. "Life is hard," she said dramatically. "You can't rely on anything. First my father was a respectable minister, and next thing I know he's a lovesick idiot talking baby talk to a woman who gets paid to sing at funerals and weddings.

"And one day my mother is my mother, wearing an apron and high-heels, and next time I look, she has a crew cut and a necktie." Daphne picked up a soggy bit of lettuce leaf, tasted it, made a face, and giggled a little.

Meredith, Sonja, and Anastasia all chuckled sympathetically.

"Sometimes," Anastasia said in a high, lighthearted voice, "someone who is a person with good values turns out to be a serious criminal, right?" She laughed self-consciously.

"Yeah, right," Daphne said. "Don't you guys change on me, okay?"

Anastasia made a decision suddenly. "I can't hang out with you guys this afternoon," she said to her friends. "I have a problem that I have to deal with. I have to go right home after school and make a phone call."

Daphne, Meredith, and Sonja all looked at Anastasia quizzically. They all knew about each other's problems. But the buzzer indicating the end of lunch period sounded, and they had to hurry. She had no time to explain, and wasn't certain she wanted to anyway.

Quickly they collected and returned their lunch trays and headed out to Mr. Francisco's class.

"Anastasia? Could you stay, just for a minute? I'd like to speak to you."

"Sure." Anastasia was gathering her books. She felt a little flattered. Mr. Francisco had never really singled her out before, although he had always seemed interested in her answers to the questions they discussed in class.

"I'll see you in the morning," Sonja whispered.

"Okay."

Anastasia waited beside Mr. Francisco's desk while the room emptied. It was very noisy until the students left; all of the eighth-graders were still arguing over the shoplifting issue. The discussion in class had been very heated. Some of the kids (mostly boys, Anastasia had noticed with a little surprise) thought shoplifting was no big deal, and that store owners should simply expect it to happen.

"You tell that boyfriend to get his act together, or you'll turn him in," Anastasia heard Mr. Francisco say teasingly to Marlene Braverman as she was leaving the room. Marlene had admitted in class that her boyfriend, a ninth-grader in another town, shoplifted all the time and that although she didn't like it much, she wouldn't dream of reporting him.

Marlene laughed and headed out into the hall; the room was quiet and empty.

Mr. Francisco closed the door and came back to his desk, where Anastasia was waiting.

"I'm kind of concerned about you, Anastasia," he said.

"Because I write wishy-washy answers?"

He laughed. "No, actually, your answers to my questions are terrific. I wish all the kids in the class would give things as much thought as you do. You seem to know intuitively that there's more to decision-making than quick, easy answers. You're good at examining things, and seeing all the different options."

Anastasia brightened a little. "But I can never make up my mind," she pointed out.

Mr. Francisco shrugged. "That will come," he said. "That's part of maturing. You guys are still eighth-graders. Of *course* you don't have answers yet. But you're beginning to see the *questions*."

"But my dad is wishy-washy, too," Anastasia confessed. "Do you think it's hereditary?"

Mr. Francisco started to laugh. "Your dad is wishy-washy? I've got news for you, Anastasia Krupnik! Did you know that I went to Harvard?"

Anastasia shook her head.

"I was an English major. I took several courses from your father: Shakespeare, and Victorian poetry, and something else, I forget what.

"And boy, does he know his stuff! I tried to bluff my way through some exams because I hadn't done the reading. I was young, then, and irresponsible. But Dr. Krupnik — I mean your father — could see right through me. He really came down hard. He flunked me in a course. I had to go to summer school to make it up.

"Think that's wishy-washy?" Mr. Francisco was grinning.

Anastasia smiled. "No," she said. "I didn't know he ever flunked anybody. He's always so *nice* at home."

"It was a nice thing to do," Mr. Francisco said, a little ruefully. "I couldn't see that until I got older. But now I can. I did a dumb thing. He didn't let me get away with it. He punished me. And I learned. Understand, kiddo?"

Anastasia nodded. "Yeah. I sure understand about doing dumb things." She sighed.

"Hey! That's why I asked you to stay — that look on your face, like you lost your last friend. Is something wrong, Anastasia? I hate to see a pretty girl like you looking so sad all the time."

Although she wished she were wearing something other than the "Surf's up" sweatshirt that her mother had brought her from a trip to Los Angeles, Anastasia felt pleased. No grown man, except her father and uncle, had ever said she was pretty before. Well, actually, Joel, who trimmed her hair occasionally at the beauty parlor on Winchester Street, said so, but she wasn't sure that counted, first because Joel was gay, but also because she paid him thirteen dollars plus a tip for a haircut, so of course he wouldn't say anything insulting.

She smiled a little. Then the weight descended once again, and her smile disappeared. Mr. Francisco waited.

Finally Anastasia said, "I did a really dumb thing. I didn't mean to. But it was illegal, and nobody knows I did

83

it, and now I don't know what to do." She could feel a small shimmer behind her eyes, as if she might cry. Quickly she bit her lip.

"Do you want to tell me what it was?"

Anastasia shook her head glumly. "I don't want to tell *anybody*," she whispered.

"Sounds to me as if you're going to have to," Mr. Francisco said. "But you know what?"

"What?"

"When you make up your mind to tell, and when you *do* tell, you're going to feel better. People always feel better if they do the right thing."

"You think so?" Anastasia, who had been staring at the floor, looked up at him.

"I know so. I *promise*."

Anastasia took a deep breath. She had made the decision at lunch, and now she renewed it in her mind. "Actually," she told Mr. Francisco, "I'm heading home right now. And I'm going to do it. I'm going to confess."

"Good for you." He walked her to the door. "When I see you in class tomorrow, you know what?"

"What?"

"You're going to be smiling. Betcha anything."

Anastasia nodded noncommitedly, and waved goodbye as she left the room. She headed down the deserted hallway. *Smiling tomorrow?* she repeated to herself. *Fat chance, Mr. Francisco. I'm probably going to be in* jail *tomorrow.*

But she headed home to do the right thing.

❖　　❖　　❖

VALUES

6. *Suppose that by donating one of your kidneys, you could save the life of your brother or sister. Would you do so?*

Absolutely. On some issues I am a wishy-washy person, but not this one. This one is easy. I would do it in a minute. For my brother, anyway. I don't have a sister. If I had a sister I would probably love her just as must as I love my brother. So I would donate my kidney to her.

Obviously if I had a brother and a sister, and they *both* needed kidneys, then it would be a problem. I read in a *National Enquirer* once about a guy who had seven kidneys, and so for him it wouldn't be a problem, he could give away several if he wanted to, but as far as I know I only have two, and I need one.

7

Anastasia leaned over the desk in her bedroom and looked at her answer to the sixth question. It had been, as she had just written, very easy. She went on to the next, even though Mr. Francisco hadn't specifically told them to.

Question seven was complicated and took her half an hour. Even then, she wasn't completely satisfied with her answer. Anastasia chewed on the end of her ballpoint pen and sighed. Maybe she would just sit here for the rest of the afternoon and do the answers to *all* the questions. It was very cozy in her room. And quiet. Sleuth was curled up at her feet, as he always seemed to be when she was home. Downstairs, Sam was puttering in his room, playing with his trucks and cars.

Her dad was at work, and her mother was folding laundry in the kitchen.

Of course she had promised herself that she would call the post office this afternoon, right after school. If she continued working on her Values questions, she wouldn't have time for the telephone call.

Anastasia sighed. "Sleuth," she said, "maybe I'll call them tomorrow, instead."

Sleuth looked up, yawned, and put his head back down on his paws.

"Or maybe I don't need to call them at all," Anastasia muttered. "What's the big deal? It's been almost a week. They've probably forgotten all about it.

"Maybe they never even noticed it to begin with."

Sleuth lifted his head and opened his eyes. Then he stood, turned completely around in a circle, lay back down, and closed his eyes again.

Anastasia read his mind. *Of course they remember. You remember and I remember. They are the ones who called the police, and who took the mailbox away and haven't put it back, and you think they don't* remember?

Come on, Anastasia, you are procrastinating, Sleuth was thinking. *And you're making excuses. You're being wishy-washy.*

The dog twitched an ear. *And also,* he was thinking, *you are disturbing my sleep.*

"All right," Anastasia said decisively, gathering her courage. She placed her paper in her looseleaf notebook and stood up. "I'm going to do it."

Her father's study was the best place in the house to make a private telephone call. Anastasia held the door open for the dog, who padded in and found a comfortable spot on the floor near the big green couch. Then she closed it tightly, went to her father's desk, sat down in his big chair, and picked up the telephone directory.

❉　　❉　　❉

"Post office." The voice, a woman's, sounded very pleasant. Anastasia took a deep breath. She had rehearsed how to begin. But it was a little like rehearsing for the Dramatic Club play at school, in which she had recently had a small role. She had said her few lines so well to her parents, and to the mirror in her bedroom, that she thought she might even be called to Hollywood or Broadway if there happened to be talent scouts sitting in the junior high auditorium for the performance. But somehow, on opening night, when the curtain came up and she could feel the presence of a lot of people sitting out there beyond the footlights, she lost her nerve — and her voice, too. She croaked her few unimportant lines sounding like a frog on a lily pad, and then trudged off the stage to take off her makeup and watch the rest of the play from the wings, feeling her theater career completely ruined.

And now she could feel it happening again. The self-confidence, the sardonic tone of voice, the sophisticated amusement at the dumb thing she had done: all of that was what she had planned and rehearsed for.

"Ah, hello," Anastasia said, and — *darn it!* — it was the frog on the lily pad again.

She cleared her throat and took a deep breath. "Could I talk to somebody about, ah, mailboxes, and what happens if you maybe put something into one that you didn't intend to?"

"What is your address?" the woman asked pleasantly. Anastasia told her.

88

"Just a moment, I'll connect you to your carrier."

"No, wait!" Anastasia croaked. She wasn't certain what *carrier* meant, but she suspected that it meant Lowell Watson. Lowell Watson was the very pleasant middle-aged black man who delivered mail to their house every day, and who had taken the time to make friends with Sleuth by giving him a biscuit after asking the Krupniks' permission. "So that he doesn't have to waste his energy barking at me when I come by," Mr. Watson had explained. "He needs to save up those barks for a burglar. Right, Sleuth?" Then he had scratched Sleuthie behind the ear and handed Anastasia's mother the mail.

Anastasia didn't want to confess to Lowell Watson what she had done. It was too gross, and he was too nice a man. He was on a bowling team, and had run the Boston Marathon once, when he was younger. And he taught Sunday School, too. How could you talk about dog poop to a person who teaches Sunday School?

"Excuse me?" the woman's voice asked.

"Um, I don't want to talk to the guy who delivers my mail," Anastasia explained, "because I'm not talking about this address. I'm talking about a *public* mailbox. I put something awful into a public mailbox." She blurted it out. She hadn't intended to say it exactly that way.

The door to her father's study opened, and Sam stood there with his thumb in his mouth, listening.

"Go away," Anastasia whispered loudly, holding her hand over the receiver.

Sam stood very still, watching her.

"*GO AWAY!*" Anastasia said angrily to her brother forgetting that she was no longer covering the receiver. "*Quit listening to me!*"

"Excuse me," the woman said, and her voice was slightly less pleasant than it had been. "What exactly is it you want?"

Sam came into the study and stood beside the couch. He looked fascinated.

"I'll call you back," Anastasia said hastily into the telephone. She hung up.

"You rat, Sam," she wailed. "You wrecked my whole conversation! I was finally decisive and said I'd donate my kidney, but now I've changed my mind! I wouldn't give you my kidney if it was the last kidney on earth! Who told you you could come in here? Who told you you could eavesdrop?"

Sam took his thumb out of his mouth. "I was just walking around," he said in an innocent voice. "What's a kidney?"

Anastasia sighed. It wasn't really Sam's fault, she knew. "Never mind," she said to her brother. "It's okay. But I want you to leave now. I have to call this person back and it's a very private phone call."

"Secret?" Sam asked with interest. Sam loved secrets, though he was no good at all at *keeping* them.

"Well, yes, it's secret," Anastasia explained. "So you go on now. Go someplace else. I'll play Chutes and Ladders with you later, after I'm finished with this."

It was the ultimate sacrifice and bribe. Anastasia hated playing Chutes and Ladders more than almost anything else in the world. The last time she had played it with Sam was when he was in the hospital recovering from an operation and she thought he might die. Actually, he had recovered just fine, and Anastasia regretted that she had played the dumb game with him. She took a vow never to do it again unless it was a real crisis situation.

Now, apparently, it was.

"Okay," Sam said agreeably. "I'll go up to my room and get it out of my toy shelf." He headed for the door of the study. In the doorway he turned just as Anastasia lifted the receiver and prepared to dial the post office phone number again.

"What awful thing did you put in the mailbox?" he asked. "I want to tell Mom about it."

Anastasia put the receiver back down. "Sam," she commanded, "get back in here and close the door. Close it *tight*."

"Sam, it's not funny. Quit laughing," Anastasia scolded him. Her brother was sitting on the couch in the study, and she had described her problem to him.

It made her mad that he was laughing. For almost a week she'd been living in the throes of guilt, terror, and despair; and her own brother found it *amusing*, for pete's sake.

Sam giggled. "Dog poop," he said.

"Yes, dog poop. And it's *not* funny. I have to call the post office, Sam, and tell them," Anastasia said. "And I want you to be absolutely silent. Can you do that?"

"Okay. I'll zip my lips." Sam made a zipping gesture, the

91

way he'd been taught in nursery school by his teacher, Mrs. Bennett. When Mrs. Bennett wanted twelve three-year-olds to be quiet, she simply announced, "Time to zip!" and the children all zipped their lips and sat still.

"Ready?" Anastasia asked. "If I dial now, and talk, you won't interrupt? You'll sit quietly, without laughing?"

Sam nodded, solemnly, his lips still zipped closed.

"And after that, it's our secret, yours and mine. Okay?"

Sam nodded.

"Promise? You won't tell *anyone*? Especially not Mom or Dad?"

Sam nodded.

"Okay. And in return, I'll play Chutes and Ladders with you any time you ask me to." Anastasia promised it reluctantly, but it was the price she had to pay, she knew, for Sam's silence.

Sam grinned, and nodded. He came back to the couch, climbed up, and sat with his feet dangling. Beneath Sam's little sneakers, Sleuth slept on.

Anastasia dialed the number again.

"This is me again," Anastasia said politely when the same woman answered the telephone. "I'm sorry I had to hang up so quickly, but I had an emergency."

"How may I help you?" the woman asked.

"Could I please speak to the head guy there? Whoever's in charge?"

The woman hesitated. Finally she said, "Please hold for a moment. I'll connect you to the supervisor."

Music began to play. Anastasia recognized the same

classical FM station that her father listened to when he was home.

"I'm waiting for the head guy to come on the line," Anastasia explained to Sam. Sam nodded solemnly.

After a moment, a man answered. "This is Austen Overholt. What exactly seems to be the problem here?" His voice was a little gruff. Anastasia bit her lip. She wanted very much to hang up. They didn't know her name. She could still hang up. It was tempting.

Then she remembered that she had given her address to the woman earlier. They could track her down. It was too late.

And also, Anastasia reminded herself, thinking of Values, *it's the right thing to do. The right thing to do should always be* easy.

And she wanted to set a good example for Sam, who was watching her with interest.

"I called to confess, Mr. Overholt," she said in a firm voice. "I tampered with the mail."

"I beg your pardon?" Austen Overholt replied. "Would you give me your name, please?"

"Anastasia Krupnik." She could tell that he was writing it down. Probably she should tell him that there was no "c" in Krupnik. A lot of people thought there was a "c".

"And what exactly did you do?"

Anastasia cringed. She had practiced and practiced how to describe what she had done. But even after practice, it wasn't easy. She had decided to start with a broad overview of the deposit and then narrow down to the specific details of the actual contents.

93

"It was last Thursday morning, early, before seven o'clock," she began.

"Last Thursday? The eleventh?" Austen Overholt repeated tersely.

Anastasia thought. "I don't remember the date," she said, finally. "I could count back. What's today? The sixteenth? Or is it the seventeenth?"

"It was *last* Thursday morning we're talking about?" Mr. Overholt asked. "Last Thursday was the eleventh."

"Yeah. It was that morning. And I was at the corner of Chestnut and Winchester, at the mailbox there — "

Mr. Overholt interrupted her. "Stop. Don't say any more."

Puzzled, Anastasia stopped talking.

"We have your address here. You are the one who called before, right?"

"Right."

Mr. Overholt read her address back to her.

"Yeah, that's right," Anastasia said.

"Krupnik? Does that have a 'c' in it?"

"No." Anastasia spelled Krupnik for him.

"And you are at that location now?"

"Yeah, it's my house. I'm sitting right here in my fath — "

"Stay right there. It will be to your advantage not to leave. Someone will be right over. Do you understand?"

Anastasia was a little annoyed. She hated it when people said "Do you understand?" as if they were speaking Chinese to her. *Of course* she understood.

"Yes," she said with an impatient sigh.

Mr. Overholt hung up without saying good-bye.

"That was weird, Sam," Anastasia said. "He didn't even give me a chance to describe the dumb thing that I did. I was going to explain about how it was my first early-morning walk with Sleuthie, and I was sleepy. Actually I thought he might possibly see that there was a little bit of *humor* to the whole thing."

Sam was listening with interest, but he didn't respond.

"You can unzip, Sam," Anastasia told him.

Dramatically Sam unzipped his lips and took a deep breath.

Sleuth thumped his tail on the rug.

"Anyway, Sam, he said someone was coming over. Can you believe that?" She stood up, went to the window, and pulled aside the curtain so that she could see the street. "He wouldn't even take my confession over the telephone."

Sleuth stood up, stretched, yawned, and came over to stand beside her. He reached his front paws to the windowsill and stood on his back legs, looking out through his fringe of hair. Sam got down from the couch and trotted over, too.

The three of them watched the street silently from the window.

"Anastasia," Sam whispered.

"What?"

"After they leave, please will you give me your kidney?"

But before Anastasia could answer Sam, Sleuth woofed at a noise from the driveway. Two police cars were pulling in.

VALUES

7. *Suppose that you got home from the grocery store and discovered that the clerk had accidentally given you a twenty-dollar bill instead of a one-dollar bill in change. Would you go back to the store and return it?*

Well, I guess I would, if the store was close by and it wasn't pouring rain. And if the clerk had been nice. Like at the grocery store we go to, the cashier is a woman named Muriel with gray hair and she always gives my brother a lollipop, after asking my mom if it's okay. So I'd give the money back to her because I wouldn't want her to get into trouble and maybe lose her job. I think she has a disabled husband, too . . .

But sometimes we go to this other store? A big supermarket? And there's a guy who works there, I don't know his name, but he's really rude to everybody. One time he yelled at my mom and made her feel really embarrassed because she had twenty-two items and she was in the twelve-or-under line, but she had done it by mistake; she didn't notice the sign. And once when Sam was standing beside me in the line, he looked down at Sam with a really glaring look and he said to me, "Don't let that kid touch the gum."

So if he gave me a twenty-dollar bill by mistake, I wouldn't give it back. Maybe I'd give the twenty-dollar bill to a homeless person, though.

8

Anastasia was back in the chair at her father's desk, but now she was feeling scared.

Her mother was there, on the couch, looking worried.

Sam was there, beside his mother, on the couch, looking wide-eyed and excited.

The only Krupnik who hadn't changed demeanor at all was Sleuth. Sleuth was once again curled up on the floor, asleep, imitating a mop.

The reason that Anastasia was scared, her mother was worried, and Sam was excited was that the rest of the room was filled with police officers. They had holstered guns attached to their belts; Sam eyed the weapons with interest.

Embarrassed, miserable, and frightened, Anastasia had told her story over and over again. One of the police officers — he seemed to be the head guy, and had introduced himself as Detective McElwain — had taken a lot of notes.

None of them even smiled when she said "dog poop."

Neither did her mother. Only Sam giggled a little each time the contents of the bag were mentioned.

Finally, when there was a pause, Mrs. Krupnik spoke up. Anastasia could tell that her mother, in additon to being worried, was also angry.

"Detective McElwain," Katherine Krupnik said, "my daughter made a very foolish blunder. She's embarrassed about it, and I don't blame her. She should have told us, and we would have called the post office immediately to explain and apologize.

"But frankly," she went on firmly, "I don't understand why the police are involved. It was an accident, but it was surely not a *crime*."

"Mom," Anastasia whispered miserably, "it was tampering with the mail. It says right on the mailbox that it's a federal crime."

"Nonsense," her mother replied. "It may be that some mail was damaged." She turned to the detective. "Was any mail damaged? Did the plastic bag *break* inside the mailbox?"

He shook his head. "The bag didn't break, ma'am." He talked the way detectives talked on TV, Anastasia observed, saying things very carefully so that they would be completely clear. She would have found the observation more interesting if she hadn't been so nervous.

"But you certainly didn't purposely damage anything, Anastasia," her mother went on. "You didn't tamper with the mail. I feel really terrible that you've spent the past few days thinking you had committed a crime.

"And," she went on, obviously warming to the task now, "I do *not* understand why you people are making such a — well, I don't want to say federal case — but such a big deal out of a bag of dog poop."

Sam giggled.

Detective McElwain smiled for the first time. "You're absolutely right, Mrs. Krupnik," he said. "And I'm sorry we've upset you and your daughter. Let me ask you this. Do you read the *Boston Globe?*"

Mrs. Krupnik shook her head. "We subscribe to the *New York Times.* We used to get the *Globe,* but my husband is a crossword puzzle nut, and he prefers the puzzle in the *Times.*"

"It was a *New York Times* bag that I used for the dog poop," Anastasia pointed out. "They're bright blue."

"We know that, ma'am," the detective said. Anastasia felt a little stupid, because of course they had known that; they were all too familiar with what she had dropped into the mailbox. But she found it a little surprising that he called her "ma'am." No one had ever called her that before.

"Well, if you people had been reading the *Globe,* this would be clearer to you," the detective said. He turned to the other police officers. "You guys can go on," he told them. "I'll finish up here."

Sam watched, wide-eyed, as the other uniformed men left the room. One of them patted him on the head and grinned. Another leaned over and scratched Sleuth.

When they had gone, Detective McElwain put his notebook away and sat down in the stuffed chair next to the fireplace.

"There's been a little about this in the *Globe* and the *Herald*," he explained, "although we've kept most of it out. Someone has been putting explosive devices into mailboxes around Boston and the suburbs."

"What's that?" Sam asked. "What's explosive devices?"

"Bombs," Anastasia told him.

"*Bombs?*" Sam asked eagerly. "*Cool!*" Sam loved bombs. He and his pals played bomb the castle, using blocks, at nursery school, although their teacher, Mrs. Bennett, didn't like it much.

"Fortunately," the detective went on, "they're home-made and *badly* made — real amateur things, with faulty timers and inaccurate wiring. And they haven't worked. But he — that is, we *assume* it's a he; statistically it's been shown that the perpetrator of an explosive device is rarely if ever a female; we were surprised to hear a female's voice on the phone saying she was confessing — "

Anastasia cringed a little, realizing what they thought when she called the post office and said that she had put something awful into a mailbox.

Detective McElwain smiled sympathetically, seeing her face. "He's getting better at it, though," he went on. "It has the possibility of turning into a major disaster. The timer worked on the last one, and it actually ignited. It singed some of the mailbox contents before it went out. But it didn't actually explode, thank goodness.

"The reason it didn't," he explained, "is because very

shortly before it ignited, someone dropped a bag of — please excuse my language, ma'am — dog doo-doo on it."

"I have to go down to the police station tonight, after dinner!" Anastasia said excitedly to Meredith over the telephone. In the kitchen, her mother was finishing dinner preparations and, at the same time, explaining the day's events to Anastasia's father, who had just arrived home. Every now and then she could hear him say, "She *what?*" It had seemed a good idea to stay clear of the kitchen for a while. So she had come into the study to call her friends.

"How come? Why do you have to go to the police station if you didn't commit a crime?" Meredith asked.

"Because the bomb was on top of a batch of mail, but *underneath* my bag of dog poop. So that means — "

"Oh, I get it," Meredith said.

"Right! I was the next person *after* the bomber to use that mailbox. They think I might actually have *seen* him."

"Or her," Meredith pointed out.

"Statistically, it's been shown that a female is rarely if ever the perpetrator of an explosive device," Anastasia explained.

"What?"

"Women don't do bombs."

"Oh. *Did* you see him?" Meredith asked.

"No," Anastasia said, a little sadly. "There wasn't anybody around. It was real early in the morning, and the only people I saw were other dog people walking their dogs. But the detective wants me to come to the station anyway,

102

to be interviewed some more, and maybe to look at some pictures."

"They'll hypnotize you," Meredith said, "to make you remember. You'll be able to tell them the license number of the car after they hypnotize you."

"What car?"

"Any car. And you'll remember your past lives, too."

Anastasia thought about that. She wasn't certain she wanted to be hypnotized. She had heard about a guy who was hypnotized and thought he was eating an orange, but really it was an onion, and he munched his way right through it and had onion breath for two days afterward.

Anastasia didn't think the police would do an onion-orange thing, but she thought she'd rather not be hypnotized unless it was absolutely necessary in order to catch the Mailbox Bomber.

"And watch out for a good cop/bad cop routine," Meredith warned.

"Yeah, I know about that," Anastasia said.

After telling Meredith good-bye and hanging up, she was preparing to dial Daphne when her father called her from the kitchen.

"Hey, sport," he said, when she appeared in the doorway. He was seated at the kitchen table, and her mother was standing at the stove, stirring something in a big kettle. "I'll take you down to the police station tonight. Mom can stay here with Sam and Sleuth."

"You're not mad?"

Her father came across the room and hugged her. Anastasia loved the feel of his beard against her cheek, even though he knocked her glasses sideways. "Listen," he said, after he'd given her a big kiss, "don't ever feel you can't tell Mom and me what's going on."

"I felt so dumb," Anastasia explained. "And scared."

"But that's exactly *when* you should tell us," her mother pointed out. "It's terrible to feel dumb, and to feel scared, but it's worse to feel dumb and scared and *alone!*"

Anastasia nodded. "Yeah," she acknowledged, "you're right."

Sam looked up from where he was sitting on the floor next to Sleuth, running a small toy car over the dog's back, lifting his ears one at a time to make shaggy tunnels, while the dog slept. "I know something worse," he announced. "Here's what's worse: if you feel dumb, and scared, and alone, and cold, and hungry, and have a stomachache, and a broken leg, and there's a robber in the basement, and a lion is coming through the door, and — "

" — and you have a deadline on book illustrations and you're not finished on time because you can't seem to get the dog's face right, " Mrs. Krupnik said.

" — and you flunked an English exam because you never got around to doing the reading," Anastasia suggested.

" — and, let's see," their father said, joining in, "how about if you completely forgot that it was Tuesday, and you didn't show up for a very important Harvard faculty meeting?"

Sam jumped up suddenly with a horrified look. "I know the *really* worst!" he wailed. "The really, really worst! How about if you were on the floor lying next to a dog and you thought your face was next to the dog's face, but it wasn't, you had the wrong end, and how about if the dog *farted!*"

They all agreed that Sam's problem was absolutely the really, really worst; and then they had dinner.

Detective McElwain met Anastasia and her father at the station and took them into a small room with a table and several chairs. Another detective, a young woman who introduced herself as Joan Sweeney, joined them.

Good cop/bad cop, Anastasia thought, and wondered which was which.

Anastasia figured that Joan Sweeney was probably the hypnotist. She looked around carefully but didn't spot any onions or oranges.

"Now all we want to do here," Detective McElwain said, "is walk through it very carefully once again and have your daughter try to describe everyone she saw that morning.

"We know that the explosive device was placed in the mailbox very shortly before Anastasia made her, ah, deposit, because we've identified the time that the mail underneath was put in. A woman who lives in the neighborhood mailed a birthday card to her mother at six-twenty-five. She was wearing a Walkman and noticed that her mother's favorite song was just starting to be played as she mailed the card, and she thought about the coincidence. We've confirmed the time of that song with the radio station.

"That birthday card — partially burned — was found

under the bomb. So the device was placed between six-twenty-five and whatever time Anastasia was there."

"Six thirty-two," Anastasia said. "I told you already. I looked at my watch right after I mailed my mom's envelope. Or I mean *thought* I mailed it. Because I was wondering whether I had time to go back to bed, and I decided I didn't."

Joan Sweeney turned a page in her notebook. "Let's go back to before you got to the mailbox, Anastasia. Which way did you approach the corner? Want to look at a map to refresh your memory?"

Anastasia laughed. "Nope. It's my neighborhood, remember? I turned onto Winchester Street at the corner of Forest Lane — "

"Wait a minute. Did you see anybody at all on Forest Lane?"

Anastasia thought hard. "No," she said, finally. "Not really. A guy came out of his house and went into his garage, after I passed. That was all, though. He was carrying a briefcase. I could show you which house, if you want."

Joan Sweeney made a note. "Then you turned onto Winchester? Going south, toward Chestnut?"

"Right."

"Any people there?"

"Yeah, a few. Let me think. A woman wearing a bathrobe came out and picked up her newspaper. Then another woman came past me, walking real fast — "

"Walking *away* from the corner with the mailbox?"

"Yeah. She had weights in her hands. She was wearing a

106

gray and white jogging suit, and she stopped, and tried to advise me what to name the dog."

"Excuse me?" Joan Sweeney looked up from the notebook.

"Well, see, I had just gotten my dog, and he didn't have a name yet, and this woman wanted to give suggestions."

"I see. Okay, moving along now, toward Chestnut — "

"Wait." Detective McElwain interrupted. "Have you named him yet?"

"Yeah. Sleuth. We named him Sleuth because it has an *oooo* sound, and his name used to be Louie, and also because he investigates everything."

The detective grinned broadly. "Great name," he said enthusiastically. "I wish I'd thought of it for my dog. I have a retriever named Fetchit."

"That reminds me!" Anastasia said. "There was a man that morning, walking two golden retrievers. But I don't see how he could have had a bomb. It was taking both his hands to keep the dogs organized on their leashes so that they didn't get tangled.

"And let's see . . . there was a guy delivering papers. But he had his hands full, too. And some joggers. Two joggers: they both said 'hi'; and there was a woman with a tall, skinny dog on a red leash. She smiled at me, and I think she said 'Cute dog' or 'Nice dog' when she looked at Sleuthie."

Joan Sweeney was writing it all down. "That all?" she asked. "Nobody else?"

Anastasia shook her head. "Nobody else. And most of those people are out there every morning. I didn't go the same way again after I, you know, after I made the mistake with the mailbox, but even when I walk the dog a different way, I see a lot of those same people."

"Well, that's a help, anyway, Anastasia. We appreciate it." She closed the notebook. "You have anything else, Bill?" She looked over at Detective McElwain.

He took an envelope out of his pocket. "Just this. A few photographs we'd like you to look at. Okay, Anastasia?"

Anastasia looked at her father. "Sure, go ahead," he said, nodding.

Anastasia expected mug shots. She expected the kinds of photographs that she saw at the post office sometimes, pictures of grim-looking people with bad hair and no chins, with WANTED printed underneath them. But glancing at the small color photographs, she saw that they were just ordinary Polaroid snapshots of ordinary people. There were six of them, all men, each wearing a U.S. Postal Service uniform. She looked through them quickly to make sure that none was Lowell Watson, who taught Sunday School and had given Sleuth a biscuit.

"Who are they?" she asked curiously. "I mean, I can see that they're mailmen. But who are they?"

Detective McElwain laid the snapshots out in a row on the table. "They're all former postal employees," he explained. "We're playing a hunch that the bomber is somebody who's mad at the post office."

"I have a confession," Myron Krupnik said. "I was mad at the post office myself, after they raised the rates last time."

"Me too," Joan Sweeney said, nodding. "But you and I didn't make bombs."

Detective McElwain positioned the photos so that Anastasia could see them clearly. "No, what I mean is someone who got fired, or who didn't get a promotion he wanted. Somebody really disgruntled."

"Makes sense," Myron Krupnik said, leaning over from his seat to look at the pictures. "Recognize anybody, sweetie?" he asked Anastasia.

She shook her head slowly, and the detective, obviously disappointed, began to gather the pictures.

"Wait!" Anastasia said. "Could I see that one again? The second one?" He handed the photo to her, and she adjusted her glasses and frowned. "I think — it's weird, but —

"Yes!" she exclaimed, remembering suddenly. "I *did* see this guy! He was right there when I scooped up after Sleuth, just before we got to the mailbox! He gave me a dirty look and I thought it was because he thought the dog was disgusting."

The detective examined the Polaroid. "What can you tell me about him, aside from the dirty look? Remember what he was wearing?"

"No, I'm sorry. I can't remember a single thing about him."

"Jeans, maybe?"

"No, plaid pants. Dark blue plaid. If you gave me an L.L. Bean catalog, I could show you what plaid. But I can't remember another single thing."

"Maybe sneakers? Nikes or something?"

Anastasia shook her head. "No. Pointy shoes. Light brown, with scuff marks. And one light brown lace, one dark brown. But I don't remember anything else."

Detective McElwain waited.

"White socks, with a brown stripe around the top," Anastasia said. "And that's all I can think of."

"Maybe a windbreaker or something? A sweater? Was it cold Thursday morning?"

"No. I was just wearing a sweatshirt jacket, the kind that zips up the front. Oh, wait! I do remember something else!" Anastasia cringed.

"Dad," she said, "I'm really sorry to tell you this. Prepare yourself for bad news."

"What?" her father asked, apprehensively.

"Ready? It's *very* bad news."

He sighed. "Ready."

"The guy was wearing a Harvard sweatshirt," Anastasia told him gently.

"Oh, *great*," Myron Krupnik groaned. "I suspected that some of my students would turn out to be criminals, but I was predicting white-collar crimes, like tax evasion. You mean I may have been teaching Shakespeare to a terrorist?"

Detective McElwain picked up the photograph and looked at the information on the back. "Nah," he said, reassuringly. "He probably got that sweatshirt at the Salvation Army store. Believe me, if he graduated from Harvard, he could've built a better bomb.

"Listen," he said, standing up, "we're going to bring this

110

guy in for questioning. You can go home now, Anastasia, you and your dad. But we might need to call you back in at some point, okay?"

Anastasia nodded. She was happy to go home, happy to have helped, happy not to have been hypnotized, arrested, fingerprinted, photographed, tried, or sentenced. She realized she was tired, too. But she wanted very much to answer question eight for Mr. Francisco's class. She would do that and then go right to bed. Sleuth would be at her bedside, woofing to go out, at dawn once again.

VALUES

8. *Suppose that you happened to be a witness to a serious crime. Would you report the criminal even if it meant your life might be in jeopardy?*

Yes, I would. Absolutely. Just as a coincidence, you asked this question at the exact same time that I happen to *be* a witness to a crime. And I've already talked to the police, and I wasn't even scared. The police were really nice, and so were my parents.

So were you, Mr. Francisco. Thank you.

P.S. Don't ever donate your old Harvard sweat-shirts to the Salvation Army. It causes a whole lot of embarrassment. My dad gives his to my mom to use for cleaning rags. And sometimes my mom wears them as a nightgown. Maybe your wife needs cleaning rags, or nightgowns.

9

"Make up your mind, Anastasia," her mother said, turning from the telephone to consult her. "Do you want to go public or not? Be famous or not?"

"I don't know," Anastasia groaned. "I guess it would be okay —"

"She says she wouldn't mind." Mrs. Krupnik spoke into the phone.

"No, wait, Mom! Do you think the kids at school would make fun of me? I don't want everybody to laugh!"

"Just a moment, please," Katherine Krupnik said to the person on the telephone. She turned to Anastasia. "Why would they laugh?"

"You know. Dog poop. It makes people laugh."

"Oh, I see. Yes, I suppose you're right. Let me see if I can — hello?" She spoke into the receiver again. "She'll agree to an interview if you'll agree not to mention the, ah, the dog excrement." She waited while the person replied. "Fine. We'll see you then."

Anastasia sighed. She wasn't certain that she wanted to be famous, under the circumstances.

"They're sending a photographer, too," her mother said

113

after she had hung up the phone. "Maybe you should go change your clothes, and comb your hair."

"Oh, *great*," Anastasia grumbled, and headed for the stairs that led up to her room. Behind her, the dog followed.

It was Wednesday evening. They had acquired Sleuth exactly one week before. Already it seemed as if he had always been a part of their family.

Tomorrow morning, Anastasia realized, it would be exactly one week since the morning she had made the mistake with the mailbox. In one way, it had been the best week of her life: the first week of having such a loving and loyal dog; but in another way, it had been the worst: all those days of guilt and indecision, planning her future in a cell block, her lifetime as a convicted criminal.

Anastasia pulled off her sweatshirt and dropped it on a chair. She looked in her closet for a clean blouse.

"Frank," she said to her goldfish, "I envy you your uneventful life. Here." She tapped a little food into his bowl, and he swam gracefully to the surface. *"Oooo,"* he shaped with his mouth, and gulped the food.

Buttoning her blouse, Anastasia could hear footsteps on the stairs. She recognized Sam's sneakers.

"Hi, Sam," she said, smiling, when her brother appeared. Then she looked at his mournful face. "Oh, dear. What's wrong?"

Sam climbed onto Anastasia's unmade bed and sat there, his expression sad, his feet dangling. "Mom did something terrible," he said.

114

"Mom?" Anastasia asked in surprise. "Don't be silly, Sam. Mom never does anything terrible."

"Yes, she did. She really, really did. I can't tell you what."

"Please?" Anastasia was curious.

Sam shook his head. "It would make you too sad."

"Give me a hint, then."

Sam thought. "Well," he said finally, "she did it to Sleuth."

Anastasia looked down. The dog was curled up on the floor. As usual, it was hard to tell which end was which; but she identified his ears, then his tail, and finally reached down and scratched his head. "He seems just fine, Sam," she reassured her brother.

"Wait till you find out what she did," Sam said. "You're going to be really, really mad."

Anastasia chuckled and began to brush her hair. She looked in the mirror over her dresser, straightened the collar of her blouse, and smiled at herself, practicing for the photographer who would be arriving soon. *Pretty nice smile*, she said to herself, hoping it wasn't a conceited thought. Mr. Francisco had said the same thing to her when she entered his classroom that afternoon. He had noticed her smiling, and had winked as if they shared a secret.

Won't be a secret for long, Anastasia thought, just as she heard the doorbell ring downstairs. The newspaper people had arrived.

❖   ❖   ❖

"No," Anastasia told the reporter. She was trying hard to sound grown up and poised, and thought she was doing pretty well. "It wasn't a difficult decision to come forward with the identification. It was the right thing to do, and the right thing is always the easiest. Don't you think so?" she added.

The reporter, a young man with ballpoint inkstains on his fingers as well as his corduroy trousers, was busy taking notes. He looked up. "What I think doesn't matter," he said politely. "*You're* the one who was responsible for the apprehension of the Mad Bomber.

"Now, could you tell me this?" he went on. "How did you happen to be in the vicinity when he placed the bomb?"

"Well, I was walking my dog." Anastasia nodded toward Sleuth, at her feet.

"And the dog's name is?"

"Sleuth."

"What breed?"

"He's a nonallergenic — "

"Wait a minute. *Nanalagic*. Okay; got it. I'll check the spelling later. Handsome dog; we'll get a photo." The reporter leaned over, patted Sleuth's rump timidly, ruffling the hair, and said, "Very intelligent face."

"That's not his face end. That's his tail end," Anastasia said politely.

"Yes, right. Now back to the Mad Bomber. Did you actually see him plant the device? Did he know you were watching? Did you feel yourself to be in danger?"

116

Anastasia shook her head. "No, actually most bomb-planters aren't violent toward individuals. See, they plant devices with timers so that the actual explosion will take place *later,* after they're gone. They're kind of cowards, to tell the truth." Detective McElwain had told Anastasia that.

"So I was probably not in any real danger," she went on, "although even if I had been, I'm absolutely certain I would have turned him in, because doing the right thing is something you can't ever be wishy-washy about, if you know what I mean."

The reporter furrowed his brow and wrote rapidly. "I'm not sure that I do," he said, "but our readers probably will.

"Now maybe you could tell me something that's sort of a human interest thing," he said. "We know, of course, that the Bomber had a real thing about the post office. What are *your* feelings about the United States Postal Service?"

Anastasia sighed, and thought. It was a question she hadn't anticipated. "Well," she said, finally, "I hate the Elvis Presley stamp."

"Over here," the photographer, a young woman with very curly hair, suggested. "By this window would be good."

Anastasia stood patiently while they adjusted the lights. She licked her lips and tried to flatten her hair a little with one hand so that it wouldn't look too messy. She hated having her picture taken even if it was just her dad taking snapshots at Sam's birthday party. But *this,* with a newspaper photographer, was *really* embarrassing. She hoped the picture wouldn't turn out too gross.

"Let's get the dog in," the reporter suggested to the photographer. "Come here, Stooge."

"Excuse me?" Anastasia said, offended. "His name is Sleuth."

At the sound of his name, Sleuth trotted over and sat by her side.

The photographer focused, then sighed. "It won't work. The dog has no face."

The reporter groaned. "I really want the dog in. The dog *growled* at the Bomber, and it's kind of the main thrust of the story."

Anastasia's mother was watching from the corner of the living room. She stepped forward. "Ah, I don't mean to interfere," she said, "but I can solve the face problem."

Sam, who was sitting on the couch watching, covered his own face with his hands. "Oh, no!" he exclaimed. "It's the bad thing, Anastasia!"

"What?" Anastasia was mystified.

Her mother came forward. "Stay, Sleuth," she said, and knelt beside the dog. "I'm sorry, Anastasia," she whispered. "I figured this out this afternoon, because I *had* to get those illustrations done."

From the pocket of her jeans, Mrs. Krupnik took two blue plastic barrettes. Carefully she clasped Sleuth's hair up off his face.

Anastasia looked down at her dog. He was clearly mortified. But he sat obediently and looked at the camera while the photographer adjusted the lens.

Anastasia read his mind. *I am a noble dog*, Sleuth was thinking. *I am descended from a long line of dogs who have served royalty, who have bestowed good fortune on monasteries, who have protected the weak, located the lost, comforted the abandoned, and fought cruelty and injustice. My forebears include Rin Tin Tin and Lassie. Therefore I am above folly. I can sit here and look noble and pretend that I do not have this asinine and ridiculous hairdo.*

"Great," the photographer said. "Now, Anastasia, put your hand on the dog's head, and I want you to try to look, oh, you know, brave and mature. Think you can do that?"

Anastasia tried. She took her cue from Sleuth, who continued to sit erect, with a haughty, dignified look on his newly exposed face.

I am Anastasia Krupnik, she told herself. *I come from a long line of Krupniks who have told the truth, who have done their homework, who have eaten their vegetables, fed their goldfish, and been kind to their younger brothers. My forebears include Myron, who was once nominated for the National Book Award, and Katherine, who illustrated a Caldecott Honor Book about elves. Therefore I am above embarrassment. I can stand here proud and tall, ignoring the fact that I am also a wishy-washy thirteen-year-old eighth-grader who threw dog poop in a mailbox.*

She touched Sleuth's head.

"Ready?" The photographer's hand was on the shutter.

"Absolutely," Anastasia said.